Star glanced over her shoulder.

Panic welled up inside as she spied Clem closing the distance between them.

The walkway filled with pedestrians the nearer she came to the center of town. On and on she ran. Her feet landed hard on the boardwalk. *Thud. . .thud. . .thud. . .*matching the rhythm of her heart as it pounded in her ears. Without slowing her pace, Star glanced behind her. *He's going to catch me.*

"Oomph." She came to a jarring halt, slammed against a rock-hard chest.

Strong hands encircled her arms in a steadying grasp. "Whoa, there, young lady. Slow down. You running from a swarm of riled bees?"

TRACEY VICTORIA BATEMAN lives in Missouri with her husband and their four children. She counts on her relationship with God to bring balance to her busy life. Grateful for God's many blessings, Tracey believes she is living proof that "all things are possible to them that believe," and she happily encourages anyone who will listen, to dream big and see where God will take them.

Email address: tvbateman@aol.com
website:www.traceyvictoriabateman.homestead.com/index.html

Books by Tracey Victoria Bateman

HEARTSONG PRESENTS
HP424—Darling Cassidy
HP468—Tarah's Lessons
HP524—Laney's Kiss
HP536—Emily's Place

But for Grace

Tracey Victoria Bateman

Heartsong Presents

To My Pastors: Matt and Aimee Flanders
I pray that God will multiply and extend to you the
abundance of grace you've poured into my life over the
past few years. I love you both.
And to the lover of my soul, Jesus Christ. Thank you
for knowing my heart and for loving me at my most
unlovable.

A note from the Author:
I love to hear from my readers! You may correspond with me
by writing:

> **Tracey Victoria Bateman**
> **Author Relations**
> **PO Box 719**
> **Uhrichsville, OH 44683**

ISBN 1-58660-773-1

BUT FOR GRACE

All Scripture quotations are taken from the King James Version of the Bible.

Our mission is to publish and distribute inspirational products offering
exceptional value and biblical encouragements to the masses.

All of the characters and events in this book are fictitious. Any resem-
blance to actual persons, living or dead, or to actual events is purely
coincidental.

PRINTED IN THE U.S.A.

one

Oregon City, Oregon 1855

Star Campbell grasped the smooth maple rail and forced her aching legs to climb the stairs. When her feet touched the landing, she breathed a silent prayer of thanks that morning had finally arrived. Wonderful, blessed dawn marked the end of another long night of dodging groping hands and avoiding leering eyes. Only a few more steps to go, then she could stretch her weary body on her cot and, for a few hours, dream of another life.

Pressing a fist to her mouth, she covered a wide yawn and proceeded down the dusty, wooden hallway until she reached the room she shared with her mother on the second floor of Luke's Saloon. She stopped short of entering as her mother's voice drifted through the closed door. "Luke, you promised."

Star frowned at the distressed tone. But it was Luke's response that made her draw back in horror.

His tone was gruff. . .mocking. "Come, now, Greta. Be reasonable. You're too old to be of use to me anymore. Star, on the other hand—she'll draw those lumberjacks like flies to a rubbish pile."

Star stifled a gasp. Leaning closer, she pressed her ear to the door.

"She's so young and innocent. Please don't do this."

"Young?" A cynical laugh erupted from Luke. "She's seventeen years old. I should have put her to work two years ago. And as for her innocence. . .do you really think she doesn't know what you're doing every night while she's serving drinks and cleaning tables?"

Heat rushed to Star's face. Of course, she knew. She hated it, but she knew.

"You've seen how the men ask for her." Luke's silky, cajoling tone made Star's skin crawl. She rubbed her arms. "They'd pay any price. Star'll be a gold mine. And you. . .well, Honey, you wouldn't have to entertain anymore. I'll even put you in charge of the other girls."

Star shrank back as the words hit her with full understanding. Luke wanted her to join the other women? He wanted her to. . .to. . . ? Panic clutched at her heart and sucked the breath from her lungs. Mama had told her over and over that Luke promised she would never have to do. . .that. That all she'd ever have to do in the saloon was serve drinks and food.

Oh, no! I just can't. . . .

"I won't have it, Luke Harper!"

Star had never heard her mother raise her voice before, but the words came out in a startling near-scream. "I followed you to every dusty town and filthy mining camp between here and California. I've done anything you've ever asked of me so that my daughter would have a better life. You promised to send Star back East to school. Or have you conveniently forgotten that promise as well as all the others you've made?"

"She's too old for that now, and you know it. It's time the girl understands what she's destined for." He gave a short laugh, completely void of humor. "Frankly, I'm amazed you'd even consider another future for the daughter of someone like you."

"Star can have her pick of good men to marry if we send her someplace where folks don't know her. Kansas City, maybe. Or New York."

"She can't hide who she is, Greta, any more than you can. Or me, for that matter. What decent man will ever want her when he finds out what she is?"

The words wound their way around Star's heart like a tight, heavy chain. Mama had always told her she wasn't made for this life—that someday the right man would come along and fall in love with her. And Star had dared to believe.

Her mother's voice drifted with finality through the closed door. "I'm sending her away tomorrow. My little girl will never sell herself to any man. Do you hear me? Never!"

A stream of curses flew from Luke's lips. Star heard a loud slap, followed by a sickening thud. "After all I've done for you, this is the thanks I get?"

A gasp escaped Star's throat. How dare he? Nearly choked with fury, she reached for the door.

"Miss Star, whut you think you's doin'?" The deep whisper stopped her before she could storm in to rescue her mother.

Star spun around, coming face to face with Luke's servant, Samson.

"Luke just hit Mama!"

"Keep yo' voice down. You want the same thing your mama's gettin' in there?"

Pushing at the massive, restraining hand on her arm, Star took in a large gulp of air and muttered an oath. "Let me go," she hissed.

"Honey, you cain't stop that man," Samson said softly. "He gots a mean streak in him a mile wide. You only get yo'sef hurt."

"I don't care. Let me go!"

"I cain't let you do it." The giant black man swept her up in his arms as though she were a child.

Kicking and fighting to no avail, Star finally fell limp against him. All of the struggle sifted from her body, and she rested her cheek against his comforting chest. He carried her down the stairs, through the deserted main room, and into the kitchen.

Lila, Samson's wife and the hotel cook, threw down a cleaning rag and pushed out her lower lip indignantly. "Sam," she said, hands on her boyishly small hips, "what you think you's doin' treatin' Miss Star like she one of dem other women? Set her down."

Samson gently lowered her to a rough-hewn wooden chair next to the table.

Leaning forward, Star wrapped her arms around herself. Great sobs wrenched her body.

"Whut's wrong, Honey? Sam, whut da matter wit' Miss Star?"

Through a haze of disbelief, Star heard Samson quietly explain her situation to Lila. High-pitched whispers followed. Heavy boots thudded on the floor, then the kitchen door opened and closed.

In an instant, Star felt Lila's comforting arms embrace her, pulling her head against a warm breast. "There, now, Chile. Everythin's gonna be a'right. Lila and Sam won' let no one hurt our gal."

She shook her head, trying to make sense of all that had just happened. "Why? Why would Luke do this?"

"Shhh, don' you fret none. Sam's goin' right now to check on yo' mama, Honey."

Relief washed over her. Samson would take care of everything.

Lila pushed a dry cloth into her hand. "Now you jus' dry dem tears, and Lila'll fix you a cup of tea."

Barely deciphering the woman's words, Star nodded, her gaze fixed on the kitchen door. Moments later, it swung open, and Samson stumbled across the room. Grabbing Star's arm, he lifted her to her feet and led her to the back door. "You gots to get outta here, Miss Star."

Fear clutched her belly at the tears streaming down the scarred face. "What is it? Where's Mama?"

"Oh, Miss Star, Luke done kilt her. I heared him telling that no-good Clem to fetch you to his office."

"No!" Star slipped through his grasp and collapsed to the floor. "Oh, no. No!" It couldn't be!

Samson hunkered down in front of her and took her face in his massive brown hands. "Honey, I knows dis be a hard thing. But if you stays here, now, you never gets away from Luke." He grabbed her arms and stood, lifting her with him. "Come on, now. Ole Sam'll get you outta here."

Helpless fury seeped through the pain and grief, bolstering Star's strength. Breaking free from Sam, she snatched up Lila's butcher knife from the counter and ran back toward the kitchen door. "I'll go to that snake's office, all right. But he'll sure wish I hadn't!"

"Put down dat knife!" Lila intercepted her, wrapping her long, bony fingers painfully around Star's wrist. "Sam's right. You gots to get outta here. You just get yo'sef in a heap o' trouble, fixin' to stick a knife in Luke. Is dat whut you thinks yo' ma'd want?"

"I—I can't just let him get away with it." Fog wrapped around her mind. Mama couldn't be gone. Lila reached forward and brushed away a strand of tear-soaked hair clinging to Star's cheek. "If Luke done kilt Miss Greta, you gots to go. You cain't help yo' mama now."

With a groan, Star let the knife clatter to the floor. She collapsed against Lila. Strong fingers grasped her arms and pushed her back. Black eyes stared firmly into Star's. "You ain't gots time fo' dis. Grievin' can come later, Miss Star. Sam, get her outta here."

Star had no strength left to fight as Sam once again took her by the arm and guided her toward the door.

"What do you think you're doing, Boy?"

Star gasped and spun around. Clem, Luke's strong-arm man, made an imposing figure standing in the doorway. A scowl twisted his face, and his burly chest stuck out as though he were itching for a fight.

"Mister Clem," Samson began, "Miss Star, here was jus' goin' out fo' a lil' while. I thought I best keep an eye on her."

Clem sneered and sized him up. "Miss Star ain't going nowheres, Boy. Luke wants to see her in his office."

"'Dat so?" Samson shuffled his feet, but kept his gaze fixed to the floor. As he did so, he inched Star closer to the back door. "When I opens de door you run lak de wind."

"What was that, Boy? You talkin' back to me?" Clem pulled back his coat to reveal his pistol.

"No, Suh. You knows I wouldn' do dat. I was jus' tellin' Miss Star she better go see Mister Luke like you says."

Fingering the Colt, Clem narrowed his gaze. His nostrils flared. "Move away, and let her by."

Samson took one step back as though he would comply. In a flash, he reached behind Star and flung the door open. "Go!" He gave her a shove.

She stumbled across the threshold and landed hard on the ground. Behind her, a gunshot rang out. Lila screamed.

Star looked back. Samson lay motionless on the wooden floor. A wailing Lila threw herself across his body. Her mournful cries rang out in the smoky, sawdust-filled air.

Oh, no. Not Sam. Star scrambled to her feet and took a step toward the kitchen, stopping at the sound of Lila's shrill voice. "Miss Star, you get outta here."

"You best stay where you are, Girl." Clem stepped away from the door and started toward her. "I can give you the same thing he got."

Anger burned inside of Star. "Samson is twice the man you'll ever be, you stinking, murdering skunk!"

"Run, Miss Star!"

"Shut up, Woman," Clem growled. With two fingers, he snatched a half-smoked cigar from his lips and tossed it to the floor, never breaking his stride. As he raised his leg to step over Samson's lifeless body, Lila grabbed his boot with both hands and pushed hard. He landed flat on his stomach, uttering curses.

Over his sprawled body, Star met Lila's dark, beseeching gaze. Star recognized the woman's silent plea. If she were caught, Sam would have died for no reason.

Clem recovered and scrambled to his feet. He sneered down at the black woman, his heavy hand poised to strike.

Through a veil of tears, Star pressed her fingertips to her lips. She extended them toward Lila as Clem's arm came down, sending the woman back to the floor with a thud. Resisting the urge to return to Lila's side, Star sprang into action and took off through the dirty alley as fast as her feet would carry her. She darted past the clutter lining the buildings and scattered in the street.

"You better stop right now, Girly!"

Desperately trying to ignore the corset cutting painfully into her ribs, sucking the breath from her body, she ran on. Her lungs felt like they were on fire as she made her way around the nearest corner.

Star glanced over her shoulder. Panic welled up inside as she spied Clem closing the distance between them.

The walkway filled with pedestrians the nearer she came to the center of town. On and on she ran. Her feet landed hard on the boardwalk. *Thud. . .thud. . .thud. . .*matching the rhythm of her heart as it pounded in her ears. Without slowing her pace, Star glanced behind her. *He's going to catch me.*

"Oomph." She came to a jarring halt, slammed against a rock-hard chest.

Strong hands encircled her arms in a steadying grasp. "Whoa, there, young lady. Slow down. You running from a swarm of riled bees?"

Star glanced up into soft, teasing brown eyes. Her heart leapt into her throat. "Wh–what?"

"Are you all right?" he asked gently.

Terror washed over her, and she craned her neck, her eyes searching for Clem. He stood, hands on his hips, only footsteps away.

"Turn me loose," she said, her voice a hoarse whisper.

A frown creased his brow, and he looked closer as though studying her. "Are you in some kind of trouble?"

"Please, it's none of your concern."

"Better let the lady go, like she said."

Star gasped at the sound of Clem's voice. "Come along with me, Star. You don't want to keep Luke waiting."

"N—no. You leave me alone. I'm not going back."

The long scar along one of Clem's cheeks whitened in contrast to the rest of his face, which had turned red as he fought to control his anger.

"Miss, are you sure you don't need help?" the stranger asked, keeping his hard gaze fixed on Clem.

Still locked in the iron grip, Star's emotions riffled between relief and hysteria.

"This is none of your affair, Mister," Clem growled. "Back off, and me and the girl will be on our way."

"It appears to me like the young lady doesn't want to go with you."

Star watched as Clem slowly fingered his pistol. With a gasp, she twisted her body, trying to break free. When the fingers tightened around her arms, she pulled back her foot and kicked hard at the stranger's leg. He let out a yowl and turned her loose.

Star darted past the man and ran as fast as she could, her ears straining for the sound of a gunshot.

When her aching legs refused to move another step, she ducked inside the livery. The smell of fresh hay and manure rose to her nostrils, causing her hollow stomach to churn. She made her way into an empty stall, hoping Clem wouldn't look that far if he was still following her. Shivering, she lifted a horse blanket from the shoulder-high partition between stalls and wrapped it around her body.

Still unable to draw a full breath, she gasped for air and wished she'd never begged Mama for a corset in the first place. Mama. The image of the precious woman who had given her life, who had raised her with tenderness and love, sent a wave of pain to Star's heart. How could the dearest, kindest woman in the world—her entire world— be dead?

The thought brought tears to Star's eyes and sapped her strength. Unable to stand a moment longer, she sank to the livery floor. She drew her legs to her chest, pressed her forehead to her knees, and gave in to her grief. When at last the tears were spent, she curled into a ball on the hay-covered floor and closed her eyes in hopeless defeat.

Despair cast a shadow over her heart. What was the point in running? She had nowhere to go. She had no friends other than Samson and Lila, and they couldn't help her now. Neither could she help them.

Weary and heartsick as she felt, suddenly nothing mattered. If Clem caught her and took her back, so what? What did she have to live for, anyway? Mama was dead. Star was all alone, with no money and no family or friends. And Luke. . .how could she have been so wrong about him? Anger coursed through her at the thought. She couldn't let him get away with murdering Mama.

The memory of Samson lying on the ground, dead from a gunshot wound, flashed to her mind, strengthening her resolve. Samson had died saving her from Clem. She couldn't let him down either. She would hide until she was sure Clem had given up looking for her. Then she'd escape once it got dark and she could slip out. She'd get away, all right. Away from the filthy saloons and men who wanted something from her that only her husband would ever have.

But escape would come later. . .after she'd rested and regained some strength. Star knew one thing for sure: If it was the last thing she did, she'd come back to Oregon City one day and give Luke what he had coming.

&

Rage simmered, then rose to a boil as Michael Riley matched the burly man glare for glare. He'd recovered from the girl's kick just in time to stretch out his leg and send "Clem" pitching to the ground before he could take out after her. The gun had flown from the man's hand and now lay in the mud, out of reach.

"Take it easy," he warned as Clem slowly climbed to his feet.

As a general rule, Michael preferred to mind his own business, but the one thing he couldn't abide was a man bullying a woman. Any woman. For any reason. Even one who had just booted the daylights out of his leg.

"Now look what you went and did, Mister," the man said through yellowed, gritted teeth. "You let her get away again."

"Seems to me, the lady needed to get away for her own protection."

The man gave him a slow, snide grin. "Don't let her pretty face fool you. That girl stole a load of cash from my boss, and he wants it back."

Michael narrowed his gaze, trying to read the expression on the man's face. "So why not go to the law?" He couldn't imagine the innocent-looking girl stealing anything, but he'd been fooled by a beautiful woman before.

"Well, the girl's like a daughter to my boss. He don't want her thrown in jail. Just wants what belongs to him."

The man strode the few steps to retrieve his pistol. Michael tensed, then breathed out as Clem retrieved a handkerchief from his pocket, wiped away as much of the mud as possible, and slipped the Colt back into his holster.

Clem cleared his throat. "Helping Star out was real gentlemanly of you, Mister, but try not to interfere with things that ain't none of your business next time. That girl's trouble." He glanced up and down the street, then locked his squinty-eyed gaze back on Michael. "Ain't no sense trying to find her now. She's likely holed up somewheres, waitin' for dark."

Releasing a heavy sigh, Michael watched him go. Unease crept through his gut at the thought of what might happen to the girl once that rough character got his hands on her, but he ignored the discomfort and excused himself with logic. He'd done all he could. The girl was more than likely long gone by now anyway. As the man had said, she was probably "holed up" until nightfall. Nothing he could do about that now. He'd tried to help her, and she'd refused his offer.

A gust of wind blew across him, sending a shiver up his spine. Michael glanced nervously at the sky. If he wanted to make it home before suppertime, he'd better get the rest of Ma's supplies and head for the farm. The way those clouds were rolling in, he knew he was in for a rough ride home.

He couldn't keep his thoughts from straying back to the girl's luminous violet eyes as he strode toward the general store, made his purchases, then crossed to the livery to pick up his horse and wagon. Even as he tried to force away the image, another face flitted to his mind. Sarah. One smile from her painted lips was all it had taken for him to fall. And fall hard. Marriage followed shortly thereafter, and then the fighting began.

He could still hear her mocking voice the day she told him she was carrying his child. "I married you to get away from Charles." Tears of anger had flowed down her smooth face. "Now I'm going to lose my figure and be saddled with a brat. I wish I had never met you! Any life is better than this."

Sarah's death during childbirth had been a sort of poetic justice. She was free from the life of a farmer's wife. Free from raising a child she didn't want. Free from the life she'd led before.

Oh, he'd known what kind of woman she was when he met her, but his heart hadn't judged. He had truly believed she wanted to change, to straighten out her tangled life. He'd been wrong. Sarah had used him the way she used all men. The only difference was, he had been fool enough to put a ring on her finger and take her home to meet his mother.

The lessons he'd taken away from his disastrous, short-lived marriage had been hard learned. But learned well, nonetheless. He would never be fooled by another woman as long as he lived.

Stepping into the livery, Michael pushed away the troublesome thoughts. Sarah had been gone for five years, but each time he allowed the memories to surface, the pain cut through him as though it were yesterday.

"Morning, Mr. Riley," Mr. Carlson, the silver-haired liveryman greeted him.

"Morning."

"Team's all hitched and ready to go, but that sky's not looking too friendly. Best wait till the storm passes."

"Thanks just the same. I think I'll settle up and be on my way." There was no telling how long the bad weather might last, and if he hurried, he might stay ahead of it all the way home.

"Suit yourself."

Michael handed the older man a couple of coins.

Mr. Carlson took the money and turned his attention to an approaching wagon outside the barn.

Michael walked to the back of the wagon and deposited his purchases among the other supplies he'd picked up the day before. Just as he started to climb into the seat, he heard a soft mewling sound coming from an empty stall. A kitten?

He grinned. Aimee had been pestering him for a kitten. Maybe it was time he surprised his little girl with the pet. Still grinning at the thought of his daughter's squeals of delight and strangling hugs, he opened the gate to the stall. The sight that met him stopped him in his tracks. That was no kitten curled up in the hay. The girl was even more beautiful than he remembered, though he wasn't sure how that was even possible.

Michael swallowed hard as she let out a soft moan and shifted. His first instinct was to turn away, get into his wagon, and ride off without giving her another thought. But something stopped him short of doing just that.

The innocence reflected in the wet lashes clinging to her tearstained cheeks and her soft, slightly parted lips melted his heart. Remembering the terror in her eyes, Michael knew there was no way he could turn her out and risk having her get caught. Whether she was guilty or not, he couldn't do it. And he had the strong suspicion God had led her to him in the first place. To what end, he hadn't the faintest idea;

clearly, she needed help and evidently God intended for him to provide it.

Gently, he bent and lifted her—blanket and all—into his arms. She moaned and opened her eyes. "You again," she whispered. "Please don't let him take me back."

"I won't."

A sleepy smile curved her lips, sending Michael's heart racing. He carried her to the wagon and laid her down among his packages. "Stay hidden," he said, raising the blanket until it covered her from head to toe. When he left the town behind, he could remove the blanket. But for now, he wanted to avoid the chance anyone would notice the dark-haired beauty asleep in the back of his wagon.

Shaking his head in annoyance at his weakness, Michael climbed up to the seat and flipped the reins. Would he ever learn to mind his own business where troubled women were concerned?

two

"C'mon."

Star woke with a jolt as strong hands closed around her shoulders and jerked her to her feet. The wagon rocked beneath her feet.

A scream tore at her throat. Clem had found her! With abandon, she began to kick for all she was worth. He was not taking her back to that saloon—not without a fight on his hands. She clamped her teeth down hard on his hand.

"Hey! Ow!" He turned her loose. "Simmer down, Lady."

Star felt no sympathy for her attacker. If she had a gun, she'd shoot him dead without thinking twice about it. Blinded by panicked rage, she wheeled around, reared back, and belted him squarely in the jaw.

Giving him no chance to finish, Star shoved hard, and he stumbled back toward the wagon gate. Gasping to catch her breath, she ventured a glance at his face. His brown eyes widened as he teetered along the edge of the wagon before crashing down to the ground. *Him!* Realizing her mistake, Star clasped a hand to her mouth.

Bewilderment registered on his handsome face as he lay sprawled on the ground, rubbing his jaw. "I can't believe you—"

A loud clap of thunder reverberated across the sky. Star screamed, instinctively covering her head with her hands while another bolt of lightning reached from the heavens, splitting a nearby tree. A crack filled the air as half the tree toppled to the ground barely ten yards from where the stranger lay.

Staggering to his feet, he shook his head as though to clear it. He stumbled to the wagon and offered her a hand.

Expecting the hand to strike, Star shrank back.

18

"Do you want to be hit by lightning?"

Star hesitated. Again, lightning flashed, followed closely by a boom of thunder. A tingle raced up her spine, causing the hairs on her arms to stand up straight. She shuddered. Grabbing the proffered hand, she hopped from the wagon and rolled underneath just as the heavens opened, sending a torrent of rain on the already damp earth. She eyed the stranger.

He cupped his jaw, rubbing the spot she'd punched. He turned to her, capturing her with a steely gaze. Then he dropped his hand and scowled.

A knot formed in Star's stomach. It was probably just as well the storm made conversation impossible. She'd likely get an earful as soon as the skies quieted.

Rain dripped through the wagon bed and slammed into their makeshift shelter from the side. Miserable, Star lay in a pool of muddy water for what seemed like hours. When the lightning and thunder moved away and the storm slowed to a gentle rain, the stranger rolled out of the shelter and looked at her expectantly.

The water soaking into Star's petticoats drenched her to the skin until her teeth chattered. With a sigh, she crawled out from under the wagon.

"I—I'm sorry for punching you. B—but you scared me."

Eyeing her, he silently rubbed his chin and jerked his head, acknowledging her apology.

"What's your name?" She lifted her skirt and squeezed, sending rivulets of water to the rain-soaked earth. "I'm Star Campbell."

"Michael Riley." He glanced her way, then gave her his back. "You're not being very modest."

Star looked down and saw her pantalets clinging to her legs. Her cheeks grew hot. She unclenched her hands and let the skirt fall. "Sorry," she muttered. "Just trying to wring it out."

"Well, let me know when you're done."

Star cringed at the frustration in his voice. "I'm done," she said, not wanting to provoke him any more than she already had, though the skirt still hung heavily from her waist.

"Fine. I'm going to care for the horses." He walked to the edge of the road where the horses were hobbled with rope and tethered to another rope that was tied between two trees.

Star admired his careful movements as he approached the skittish animals. Speaking in low tones, he stroked first one, then the other. Moments later, when he walked back to her, he gave her a tight smile.

"We can be thankful the only tree hit was that one over there," he said, inclining his head toward the road ahead of the wagon.

She nodded. He regarded her as though he expected her to comment, but Star couldn't think of anything to say. He adjusted his hat and, with a shrug, made his way to the fallen tree. Each step was smooth and confident, inviting Star's admiration.

His irritation with her had been evident, but Star could tell he wasn't the type to be violent. She knew a lot about men, and she'd wager a night's tips he wouldn't hit a woman, no matter how she provoked him. Still, she didn't want to anger him, she wanted to help him—to repay the kindness he'd shown her thus far.

Star watched as he struggled to lift the tree. She joined him, grabbing hold of the other end.

"What do you think you're doing?"

"Obviously, you'll never get this thing out of the road by yourself," she said with a grunt. "I want to help."

Michael sent her a scowl. "Do you think we're going to lift the whole tree?"

Brow lifted, Star blinked. That was precisely what she'd thought. "What were you trying to do?"

"Come here, and we'll try to lift this end together. Maybe we can turn the thing around enough to get the wagon past."

Without a word, Star moved to his end of the massive half-tree.

"All right. On three, lift."

She did. But the monster refused to budge.

After three tries, they had made no progress whatsoever. Michael growled and gave it a sound kick.

"That must have really hurt that old tree." Star rolled her eyes. Men!

He gave her a sheepish grin, sending her pulse racing. "It made me feel better."

"What are we going to do now?" A knot formed in her stomach. "Y—you're not going back to Oregon City, are you?"

"Don't plan to."

Relief flooded Star, and she sank down wearily onto the tree.

Breathing heavily from the exertion, Michael straddled the trunk, facing Star. He yanked off his hat, revealing thick, reddish-brown hair plastered to his head from a combination of rain and sweat. Star tried not to stare, but she found the scruff of a beard lining his jaw only added to this man's appeal in a way that made her heart race.

"What were you doing, hiding in that stall?"

"What do you think I was doing?" Star retorted more sharply than she'd intended. She couldn't help but be bewildered by her reaction to this perfect stranger. Many men had tried to catch her eye over the last few years, but none had been successful. That this stubborn, difficult man could send her heart into a tizzy bothered Star no end.

Apparently taking no offense to the sharpness of her words, he simply nodded. "Don't you have any friends? Family? Someone who would have taken you in?"

"If I did, do you think I would have hidden in a barn and covered myself with a smelly, old horse blanket?"

"Are you always this sharp-tongued when people try to help you?"

Star bit back a retort. For now, she was at this man's mercy, and it was pretty evident he was tiring of her. "I'm sorry," she murmured. "I do appreciate your help. After I kicked you, I wouldn't have blamed you if you'd left me in that horse stall." She cut her glance to him. "Why'd you carry me out of there, anyway?"

His brow lifted, thoughtfully. "I'm not really sure. Maybe God led me to do it." He shrugged. "Who knows?"

God? A thrill passed over Star's heart. *Oh, Mama, if only you could have lived to see that I was right about God. He does care about the likes of us.*

Tears sprang to her eyes at the thought of her mother. Never again would she lay her head on Mama's lap and feel gentle hands rubbing her hair. With whom would she share her secrets now? She longed for solitude so she could cry out her anguish.

"What's wrong?" Michael asked.

Star glanced up, noting the bemused frown on his face.

"Nothing," she replied, blinking back the tears clouding her vision. It wouldn't do to show her tears and elicit questions from him. She needed to distract him before he got nosy. Mustering the energy, she turned her prettiest smile on him. "Except that I'm so happy you stuck out your neck for me. Just think, I might have ended up being found by someone who isn't nearly as charming and helpful as you are."

With a short laugh, he sent her a dubious look. "Save your flirting. It's wasted on me."

Star's cheeks burned. So flattery only worked on some men.

She decided to change the subject. "Is your farm near a town?"

"Why?"

"I'll need to find a position somewhere."

He scrubbed a hand over his face and winced when it made contact with his jaw.

Star sucked in a breath. Hopefully, the painful reminder of her attack wouldn't break the peace between them.

"Hobbs is a couple of miles from my farm, but there isn't much to the town. We just built a church. My brother's the preacher." Pride shone in his eyes. "We'll use the building for the school too, soon as we find a teacher. There's a small mercantile." He gave her a wry grin. "Not much of one, but it'll do in an emergency. Let's see, what else? One of my neighbors is talking about opening a lumber mill, but he hasn't made up his mind yet. Joe Grafton's restaurant is always needing someone to serve the food, but Joe's a pretty rough character from what I understand. Keeps running off the help. I guess that's about it. Unless you know anything about blacksmithing or shoeing horses." He laughed at his own joke.

Star's heart sank. The only position available to her was to serve food? Exactly the kind of job she wanted to avoid.

"I—is that the only town nearby?"

" 'Fraid so. Other than Oregon City. But that's a good half day's ride." He sent a wary look toward the sky. "When the weather cooperates."

"Well, that's not an option, anyway."

"Didn't think so." He eyed her reflectively. "Do you want to tell me why that man was chasing you?"

Star averted her gaze to her fingers. Now what? She tried to think up a good lie, but as always, her mind went blank. She fumbled with her hands as the silence grew incredibly loud between them.

"Never mind. You don't have to tell me anything." Michael stood suddenly, swinging his leg over the tree. "I'd better hook the team up to a chain. Looks like ol' Pete and Dan are going to have to pull this monster out of the way if we're to make it to the farm by nightfall. I don't know about you, but I'm looking forward to the hot meal waiting for me."

Hot meal? Star's heart sank. Of course he must be married. He was at least twenty-five years old by her estimation. Someone would have snatched him up by now. She felt foolish, remembering her racing pulse when he'd smiled at her.

"How will your wife feel about you bringing a woman home?" she called after him.

"I doubt she'll care since I don't have a wife," he replied over his shoulder.

Star stood and followed him to the wagon. "But you said. . .well, then who is going to have a hot meal waiting for you?"

"My ma." Without looking up, he began to work with the team.

"Do you mean to tell me you still live with your mother?"

He shot her a quick glance and scowled. "No," he said in a clipped tone. "She lives with me."

Star groaned inwardly. Mothers could sniff out a woman of questionable character a mile and a half away. And they couldn't be sweet talked, either. She'd be tossed out on her backside before she could say, "Howdy do." Star muttered an oath.

"What did you just say?" Michael asked incredulously, straightening to his full height.

She repeated the word.

"Lady, you have a dirty mouth."

"Dirty? I only said. . ."

"I heard you, and don't think you can talk your way around this issue. I have a five-year-old daughter at home, and I will not have her exposed to such foul language."

Foul language? Star gaped at him. "Do you mean—?"

He stepped back, holding up a hand, palm forward. "Don't say it again."

He strode to the other side of the wagon, leaving Star to stare after him in bewilderment. She caught up to him, her long legs matching his, stride for stride. "What do you mean you have a daughter? I thought you said you weren't married."

"My wife died when Aimee was born."

"Oh," Star mumbled. "I'm so sorry."

He shrugged. "Don't be. She's not."

"She's not what? Dead?" Michael was sure an odd duck. Did he have a wife, or didn't he?

Michael took a step, then stopped as Star blocked his path. "She's not sorry she's dead. Okay?"

"I don't understand."

"She didn't want to live if she had to live with the likes of me. All right?" He took her by the arm and moved her out of his way. He grabbed one horse by the bridle and led the team toward the fallen tree.

Spurred on by insatiable curiosity, Star trailed behind him, refusing to be intimidated by his frustration. "Well, how could you possibly know that?" Confused by the whole conversation, she felt a measure of hope all the same. "Do you have the power to speak with the dead?" she asked in a hushed voice.

"What?"

"You know. . .the power to converse with the dearly departed." Star had visited a traveling carnival once where a lady claimed to have the power to tell the future and communicate with the dead. At the time, there was no one she especially felt the need to speak to—not enough to part with ten cents, anyway. Star gathered a deep breath, suddenly feeling foolish. But, if Michael knew how his wife felt about being dead, he must have been talking to her about it. "Well?" she asked, resting her hands firmly on her hips. "Can you or can you not speak with the dead? Or is your wife the only person you can conjure up?"

His jaw dropped, his eyes wide in horror. "What are you suggesting?"

Stung by his sharp tone, Star felt heat rise to her cheeks. "I just. . .well. . .will you help me speak to my mother?"

"How can I?"

Unbidden, tears filled her eyes. "She was. . .that is, she died recently, but I didn't have a chance to say good-bye." Her voice was a hoarse whisper. "If I could only speak to her one more time."

All the thunder left his face. He dropped the bridle and took Star's hands in his.

She eyed him warily and pulled away from the warmth of his touch.

He didn't try to hold her, but placed two fingers beneath her chin, raising her head gently until he captured her gaze. The kindness in the brown depths surprised her, confused her, and made her want to lay her head against his broad chest and unburden herself.

"Honey, no one can speak to your ma after she's dead. The Bible is very clear that to even try is sinful. Worse, it's an abomination to God."

"It is?" Star didn't want to be sinful or an abomination—whatever that was. She wanted desperately to be good. Ever since the night she'd learned about Jesus from an old drunken miner, she'd tried to be kind and obedient—to somehow make up for all the pain Jesus had gone through at her expense. She didn't own a Bible, had never even seen one up close, but, oh, how she wanted to please God. "S–sinful?"

He gave her a solemn nod. "I'm afraid so. Didn't you know that?"

Feeling foolish, Star felt her defenses rise. "Well, if I knew, do you think I'd have asked about it?"

"How am I supposed to know? So far, I've noticed you don't seem too concerned with what is or isn't right. You kick and punch perfect strangers trying to help you, you use foul language, and you raised your skirt when I was looking right at you. I'm not sure what kind of woman you are."

A gasp escaped her lips. "How can you say that? You don't even know me." An image of women turning away from her mama on the street flashed through Star's mind, igniting her anger. This man was no different from the people in town who crossed the street when she and Mama came anywhere near, people who never had a kind word for the likes of them.

Familiar resentment burned inside of Star until she felt she might burst. A torrent of words bubbled to her lips as she opened up and let him have it. With an eloquence she didn't know she possessed, Star released all the pent-up frustration she'd held onto for years. Frustration of being turned out of school after school when people—usually the very men who frequented the saloons—found out she was attending with their precious children.

The bewilderment on Michael's face gave her some measure of satisfaction as she told him just what she thought of his high-and-mighty attitude.

His brow furrowed when she called him a hypocrite. And his eyes grew stormy when she told him she'd met a huge grizzly bear with more kindness than he would ever possess.

Then the moment came when she knew she crossed the line. The words flew from her mouth before she could stop them. "And no wonder your wife would rather be dead than stuck living with an unfeeling, grouchy man like you."

three

Michael felt the blood drain from his face. How could such beautiful lips utter the cruel words he had just heard? Pain knifed through his heart, and suddenly he felt weak. Unable to speak, he stared in stunned silence at the flushed face before him.

Her eyes grew wide and her hands flew to her mouth. "Oh, Mr. Riley," she said, her voice full of regret. "I don't know how I could have said such a horrid, horrid thing."

Michael grabbed a chain from the bed of the wagon and walked back around to the horses. "Forget it. It doesn't matter."

She trailed behind him. "Of course it matters. You've been nothing but kind and helpful."

He maneuvered around her to attach the chain. "And so far it's gotten me punched, kicked, bit, and a good tongue-lashing," he said bitterly. "You certainly know how to show your appreciation."

"You're right. I don't deserve your kindness."

The self-loathing in her voice melted some of Michael's anger. Some. But enough remained to keep him from falling for the quivering rosy lips and eyes luminous from the tears. He'd been taken in by such beauty before. This woman had been nothing but trouble since he'd met her. Her recent poisonous words solidified his suspicion that she was just as cruel as Sarah. Was there not a lovely woman alive who was lovely in spirit as well? Or must a man choose between beauty and grace? If a man gave in to the lust of the eye and fell for a pretty face, was it his lot in life to be saddled with a sharp-tongued shrew? Well, not him. That was for sure. If he had to marry the ugliest woman God ever made, he'd see to it Aimee had a decent woman to call "Ma." A God-fearing, sweet tempered gal who would love him the way a man needed to be loved.

Michael led the horses to the fallen tree and found a branch he hoped would be thick and sturdy enough to drag from.

"I—is there anything I can do to help?"

"No." He wrapped the chain securely to keep it from slipping. "Just stay out of the way. I've wasted enough time as it is."

From the corner of his eye, he saw her shoulders drop as she walked away. Guilt pricked him, but he brushed it aside in a moment of indignant self-justification.

After all, he had left home two days before, expecting to sell a pig and pick up enough supplies to last a few weeks. Everything had gone as smoothly as he could have hoped for until this slip of a girl had smacked into him. Now he was stuck with her—a foul-mouthed little heathen who, in all likelihood, would rob him blind in his sleep.

Fighting with the horses as they slipped around on the muddy road, Michael turned his full attention to the chore, all but forgetting about Star in the process. When the tree finally lay at the side of the road, he looked around. The girl was nowhere in sight. His throat tightened. Where could she have gone? A good thirty minutes had passed since she walked away, so she couldn't have gotten far.

He assessed the situation. There were only two choices for her: the woods or the road back to the very place she had run away from.

If he were a betting man, he'd wager a nickel she'd head back to town and try to find another way to avoid being caught. Most likely, another unsuspecting man would take pity on her before the day was out. Good riddance.

If she doesn't get herself caught first.

Frustrated, Michael yanked off his hat and wiped the sweat from his brow with the back of one hand. Why should he care if she walked all the way back to Oregon City and faced what she had coming for stealing? He wasn't wasting any more time on her. He'd hitch up the wagon and head for home.

He set about doing just that, trying to ignore his niggling conscience, until finally in frustration, he smacked his hat against his thigh and stared heavenward.

"But that girl is nothing but trouble, Lord," he argued. "Look what she's put me through in the few hours I've known her."

A leftover rumble of thunder in the far distance answered. He couldn't very well just leave her on the road alone—even if she did deserve it.

Releasing a heavy sigh, Michael climbed into the wagon. The girl obviously needed help—the kind of help only God could give her. Resolutely, he turned the horses to the road heading back to Oregon City.

Within a few moments, he spied Star ahead of him. She looked so fragile, walking between the trees towering above her on either side of the road. A protective urge tugged at Michael's heart, and suddenly he was glad he'd followed her.

Star glanced around.

Michael waved.

Jutting her chin, she turned back to the road and straightened her shoulders without slowing her gait.

Look, Lord, she's not even grateful I came after her.

Michael flicked the reins, and the horses quickened their step. Within a couple of moments, he was close enough behind her that the horses could have nudged her if they'd wanted to. He cleared his throat loudly, waiting for her to acknowledge his presence. She ignored him.

"Get in the wagon, Star. You know you can't go back to Oregon City. What about that rough character looking for you? Do you want him to nab you?"

"It's no more than I deserve for speaking to you the way I did."

Michael didn't try to cover his smile. He inched the wagon beside her. "Come on," he said, as though speaking to his daughter. "Let's go home."

"I don't have a home," she said with a sniff. Michael could see the tears creeping down her face, and his heart lurched.

"You can stay with us until you figure out what to do," he offered. Now where in the world had that come from? He'd planned to let her stay the night, then take her into the small, nearby town of Hobbs in the morning. He figured she could work in the restaurant.

"I don't take charity." She lifted her chin. "I'd rather go back and face Luke."

You'll take money that doesn't belong to you, but not a little kindness that's freely offered? He kept the words to himself. She had no idea he knew what she'd done. If there was any hope for her soul, he'd have to wait until she repented and confessed her sin on her own.

"Glad to hear it, because I'm not suggesting charity. You can work for your keep until you find something else."

That stopped her in her tracks. Her brow creased. "Listen, Mister, I know you don't have a wife, but I'm not that kind of woman."

"I don't know what you mean," Michael replied, pulling the horses to a stop.

She eyed him warily for a moment. Her eyes grew wide, and a bright pink spot appeared on each cheek. "Oh."

Understanding dawned on Michael. He felt the heat creep up the back of his neck and knew his face was as red as hers. Where had the girl gotten such crude notions?

Are you sure I'm supposed to take her in, Lord? What about Aimee? I don't want this woman teaching my daughter sinful habits.

"All I meant was that my ma is getting on in years. She could use a little extra help around the place. And that's all."

"No, thank you. I don't deserve your kindness."

Michael expelled a heavy sigh at her dramatics. If she kept up the self-loathing, she'd end up in sackcloth and ashes before the day was out.

He hopped down from the wagon and reached out. "Come on. You know you can't go back to Oregon City. And you'd be doing me a mighty big favor if you come help Ma out."

She released a sigh and remained silent a moment as though weighing her options. Then she nodded. "All right." Avoiding his gaze, she accepted his hand and climbed up into the wagon. She scooted as far away as she could without falling off the seat.

Michael shook his head and climbed up beside her. Carefully, he flicked the reins and maneuvered the horses around.

As he headed the wagon toward home, anxiety gnawed at his stomach. How would he ever be able to explain this to his mother?

❧

"Wake up. We're home."

From a dream world, Star awoke to the soothing voice. Slowly, she came to consciousness, aware of her aching cheek. Her eyes flew open as she realized her head rested upon Michael's solid shoulder. She jerked away, heat rushing to her face. "Sorry," she muttered. "Why didn't you wake me up sooner?"

"I'm surprised you slept at all, the way this wagon bounced and slid around in the mud," Michael said with a chuckle.

Star held herself up primly and settled her hands in her lap. "Well, it's just not very proper for me to have rested my head on your shoulder like that. It's bad enough we didn't make it to your home before dark."

Star groaned inwardly. What would his mother think? Would she be like the town women, all propriety and no kindness? Probably. The very thought filled her with dread.

Michael leaned toward her, causing Star to shrink back. "Don't worry," he said in a conspiratorial tone. "I won't tell a soul."

Michael pulled on the reins, and the wagon slowed to a stop. He hopped to the ground and offered her a steadying hand. "Go on up to the house while I unhitch the wagon and put the horses down for the night."

Star's stomach tightened. "N—no, I'll wait for you." If she went to the door alone, the woman would send her packing before Michael even made it up to the house.

Michael shrugged. "Suit yourself."

A shiver slid up Star's spine as he led the horses to the barn, leaving her alone in the black, starless night. Nervously, she rubbed her hands up her arms. She hugged herself tightly for warmth, wishing for her shawl.

The overwhelming events of the day came rushing back. Everything she'd ever known was gone. She was orphaned, without a stitch of clothing besides what she wore on her back, and so little money in her pocket, she couldn't afford to buy any more. And here she was, at the mercy of strangers.

Oh, what had she been thinking? This Michael Riley could be a robber or a murderer. She might be worse off now than she'd been in Luke's greedy clutches. *And what if. . . ?* Star gasped at the wretched thought spinning around her brain. What if Michael didn't have a mother or a daughter? What if that was only a ploy to get her to come all the way out here?

Panic gripped her. She turned on her heel and fled into the night, back up the rutted road leading away from the house. She didn't care where she ended up, but anywhere certainly would be better than being stranded alone with a lying skunk like Michael Riley.

Star stumbled along blindly, praying for all she was worth that no wild animal would capture her scent and come to investigate.

She glanced around and screamed as a shadowy figure closed the distance between them. Without warning, her foot twisted painfully, and she lost her balance. The ground came up to meet her, and she landed with a squish on the muddy road.

Pain shot through her ankle. Star moaned, knowing there was no way she could outrun whatever was chasing her. She rolled over, prepared to fight off the attacker. Before she could put her hands up in defense, a furry body straddled her. Massive paws rested on her chest, pushing all breath from her body. She looked up at sharp, white fangs. Closing her eyes, she waited to become dinner for the beast.

A warm tongue lapped at her face.

"Cannonball, get your muddy paws off the lady."

Star's eyes popped open at the sound of Michael's voice. She took a closer look at the wild beast and nearly fainted in relief. Cannonball turned out to be a big, tail-wagging mutt. He licked her a couple more times, then let out a loud bark.

Michael laughed outright. "You made his night. It isn't often old Cannonball gets someone new to play with."

Star ignored his outstretched hand and struggled to her feet. But her ankle gave out, and she would have lost her footing again, if not for Michael's sudden, steady hand on her arm. "I wasn't playing with him. I was running away from him."

"Well, don't let him hear you say that," Michael said, amusement thick in his voice. "You might hurt his feelings."

Cannonball sniffed her hand, then gave it a lick, leaving a wet streak. Star pulled away and rubbed her palm on her skirt. "As if I'm worried about hurting his feelings," she huffed, pushing at the great mutt as he jumped up on her, nearly sending her back to the ground.

"Down, Boy," Michael said sternly. His hand tightened around her arm, and he started to guide her back up the road toward the house.

Star sucked in a breath as she tried to step down.

"Did you hurt yourself?"

"My ank—foot."

"Put your arms around my neck."

"Th—that won't be necessary."

Michael released a heavy, frustrated sigh and swung her up

into his arms before she could resist.

"I can walk!"

"I doubt it. And even if you could limp your way up to the house, it would take twice as long. As I told you hours ago, I'm hungry."

Star's stomach did a flip-flop at her closeness to this man. She tried to dredge up the anger she'd felt just moments before, but his warm breath tickled the arm she had slung around his neck for support, making it impossible for her heart to harden against him.

Excited by the new game, Cannonball let out a high-pitched bark and jumped up again, knocking against Star's ankle. "Ow! That's the worst dog I've ever seen in my life. Can't you make him stay off me?"

"Bad dog," Michael said, lowering his tone. "You're hurting Star. Now you stay down."

Miraculously, the animal obeyed.

"You know," Michael said. "If he scared you, you should have run to the barn instead of heading off down the road. You could have gotten lost if you'd run into the woods."

"I didn't think," Star muttered, unwilling to admit she had been running away from the man and not the beast, to begin with. A quiver rippled through her stomach. What would she find when they got inside?

❧

This girl was nothing but trouble. Bad enough he had to explain her presence to his mother. Now he also had to try to explain why she was caked in mud from head to toe.

He knew better than to question God again. For some reason, this waif had been led to him. All he could do was try to find a way to help her.

Michael stepped onto the porch. Star sighed, her breath against his neck sending a rush of emotions through him.

Turning, he looked into her heart-shaped face. The lamp hanging over the awning cast a glow over them, making her hair shimmer in the light. Even with her face smeared with mud, her beauty shone through.

He lifted his eyes to meet her gaze. His breath caught in his throat at the fear widening her eyes. She was afraid of him? All he had done since he'd found her was try to help her. How could she even imagine he'd do anything to harm her?

He would have demanded an answer, but the door swung open. His mother stood at the threshold, wearing a relieved smile. "Michael, you're home! I was beginning to worry. My word, who have you got there?" She moved back.

"This is Star Campbell," he said, stepping inside.

"Y—you really have a ma?" Star squeaked out.

"Of course I have a—"

"What did you do to the poor child? She's covered in mud."

"It was that mutt. He—"

"Daddy! What took you so long?" Aimee stood in the center of the room, looking very much like a doll in her nightgown and lacy nightcap.

"Hi, Sweetheart—"

"And a daughter?" Star began to sob.

Ma jammed her fists onto her round hips. "Now look. You've gone and made the sweet thing cry."

Michael's head whirled from all the questions flung at him. Star thought he had been lying to her? That explained her fear.

"Shh, Star. Everything's all right now," he said, wishing the wailing in his ear would stop.

"Come," his mother said. "Let's lay her down on my bed."

"She's filthy. How about the cot in the lean-to?"

"Don't be ridiculous," she retorted. "It's dusty and cold out there."

Michael sighed heavily. "She can take your room, and you can use the loft. I'll sleep in the lean-to for tonight."

Star let out another loud sob. "I can't take your bedroom, Ma'am!"

"Nonsense. You'll just use Aimee's bed, and she'll hop in my bed with me. We gals can all share that one room, and Michael can keep to his loft."

"You can stop arguing over where to put me," Star gulped, "because I'm not staying."

"Of course you're staying," Ma said firmly, gentleness softening her voice.

"I don't want to be any trouble, Ma'am. I've already caused your son more than his share."

Ma patted her arm gently. "Don't you worry yourself about any of that. Michael can take it." She cast her gaze upward. "Now, go set her down in a chair by the table, and I'll warm some water for a nice bath."

Star swiped at her nose with the sleeve of her dress, smearing more mud on the perky tip.

Fearful of sending her into another tizzy, Michael fought the urge to laugh aloud at the sight.

Ma turned her attention toward Aimee, who scampered around the room, trying to assess the situation. "Aimee, Honey, you can sleep with me tonight, and we'll let our lovely guest sleep in your bed. How does that sound?"

"Okay."

Michael's mother scurried to the kitchen.

Aimee cast a shy glance up at Star. "Don't you wish sometimes you could just keep the mud on for awhile? Grammy always wants me to wash it off right away."

Star sniffed and giggled. The sound captured Michael's heart. It was the first time he'd heard her laugh. The spontaneity was every bit as heartwarming as a child's.

"I've never been covered in mud until now," she admitted.

The little girl gave her a serious look. "How do you like it?"

Star's lips twitched, and Michael could tell that she was trying to keep her expression grave to match Aimee's. "Well, it's not too bad," she said. "But I think I prefer to be clean."

Aimee sighed. "I suppose it's because you're grown up." Her face lit with a grin. "I like being muddy better."

"Run along and do as you were told, Sweetheart," Michael instructed. "Crawl into Grammy's bed. I'll be in to hear your prayers soon."

"Yes, Pa." Aimee bobbed her little head, wrapped a quick hug around Michael's leg, and set off to do as she was told.

"Sorry about that," Michael said.

"About what?"

"She's rather outspoken."

Star's lips curved into a soft smile. "I think she's sweet." She cleared her throat, her eyes downcast. "Mr. Riley, I'm sorry I doubted you."

Michael started toward the table. "You don't know me well enough to trust me yet. Let's forget about it for now, okay?"

Star winced when he set her down. Sliding a chair up close, he gently lifted her leg and propped her foot. "May I take a look at it?"

A blush crept to her pale cheeks. She nodded her assent. Quickly, she averted her gaze, which was just as well. His attraction for her was growing, and he didn't need the complication of being captured by her luminous eyes. He could either have a beautiful woman or a proper mother for his daughter. They just didn't come in the same package. For Aimee's sake, he had to be practical. If he had to throw on a blindfold every time he walked into the same room with Star, so be it. He wouldn't be hornswoggled again.

Grabbing her dress with both hands, Star inched the skirt upward, revealing tattered slippers. Michael could only wonder why she would wear such impractical footwear, but in this case, it was a mercy. Michael would never have gotten a boot off her foot without causing her undue amounts of pain.

Gingerly, he lifted her heel. Star drew a sharp breath. Michael glanced up. Her lip was captured between her teeth, and fresh tears of pain shimmered in her eyes.

"I know it hurts, but I have to get the shoe off."

She nodded. "It's all right."

Michael slipped it off as gently as he could, but knew from her furrowed brow and deathly white face, the pain was excruciating.

She let out a long, slow breath once he set her foot back on the chair.

Ma bustled to the table, carrying two heaping plates. "You both must be starving." She glanced at Star's foot. "What happened?"

"She twisted her um. . .limb outside." Michael scowled. "Why did you think I was carrying her?"

Ma shrugged. "Well, how was I to know? I thought maybe you'd gone and found yourself a wife."

Feeling the heat scorch his ears, Michael cleared his throat. "No, Ma. Cannonball scared the daylights out of her, and she hurt her foot running away from the dumb mutt."

Ma scowled and set the plates down on the wooden table. "That animal. He's going to be the death of someone one of these days. I should've sent him packing long ago."

Michael couldn't help the grin playing at the corners of his lips. Ma had found the dog as a pup and insisted they take him in. She spoiled him more than any of them. Of course, he couldn't very well remind her of the fact, or he was liable to get a thwap on the head.

"Please don't send Cannonball away," Star pleaded. "It was really my own fault, anyway. H—he thought it was a game."

Ma's face softened, and she reached out a plump hand to pat Star's arm. "All right. He can stay." She turned her gaze to Michael and sharpened her tone. "But teach him some manners."

"Yes, Ma."

"Now, you two eat before your supper gets cold," she ordered. "I'll sit here and drink my coffee, and you can tell me all about how you came to find each other."

Star jerked her head up, sending Michael a silent plea.

Michael wanted to respect her obvious wish to keep secret the fact that someone was after her, but he knew he couldn't keep the truth from his ma. Not only was it the wrong thing to do, it wasn't possible. Ma could smell a lie from ten miles away.

He gave Star a reassuring smile and launched the tale.

"What were you running from, Honey?" Ma asked when he finished.

Star kept her gaze on her plate.

Ma reached over and took the girl's hand. "It's all right, Star," she said gently. "You'll tell us when you're good and ready. Until then, don't you worry. You're safe with us."

"Thank you, Ma'am."

"You must call me Miss Hannah. Everyone does." She stood and headed for the stove. "Now, that water should be just about ready. Son, can you go and get one of Sarah's old night shifts so Star can have a bath and get to bed? She looks exhausted."

Michael stiffened at the suggestion. He hadn't touched Sarah's clothing since he'd packed them away after her death. The thought of Star wearing any of Sarah's frilly things irritated him and brought back his suspicions. Were these two women cut from the same cloth?

Star glanced quickly at Michael. "I. . .really don't bother," she said. "I don't want you to go to any trouble because of me."

Ma waved away the protest. "Nonsense. It's no trouble at all. Those clothes are just packed away in an old trunk up in Michael's loft. Anything I own would wrap around your little body three times." She looked pointedly at Michael. "There's no choice."

She was right. The poor girl had to have something to wear. But he made a mental note. First thing in the morning, he would go to the mercantile in Hobbs and buy material for her to make some things of her own. As soon as she did, he would burn every last stitch of clothing Sarah had owned.

"Will you be all right in here alone for a few minutes?" Ma asked.

"Yes, Ma'am," Star whispered, without looking up. Ma fixed her gaze back on Michael. She raised her brow, and he braced himself for the kind of tongue-lashing only Ma could give.

"Come onto the porch and help me carry in the washtub, Son," she said pointedly, allowing for no objections.

Michael followed her outside. As soon as the door shut behind them, she whipped about, hands resting on ample hips.

"How could you make that child feel so unwelcome?"

Michael blinked in surprise at the attack. "Unwelcome?"

"You nearly refused to allow her to wear Sarah's things. Your wife has been gone for five years. It's high time you start living again. That sweet thing in there needs us, and I intend to make sure she feels just as welcome as if she were the president's wife. And so will you, or so help me I'll. . ." Her eyes widened, and she reached out to touch his bruised jaw. "Michael! What happened to your face?"

Still reeling from the onslaught, Michael laughed outright. Bending way down, he kissed her plump cheek with a resounding smack. "That sweet, helpless thing in there knocked me flat on my back. That's what. And you ought to see the bruise on my leg from the kick she gave me."

He couldn't help but enjoy the effect his words caused. Ma gaped at him, her eyes round as saucers. "She did that to you?"

" 'Fraid so." He grew serious. "Ma, the man who was chasing her told me she stole a load of cash from her guardian. I know God sent her to us, but we need to use wisdom so we don't get ourselves robbed."

Ma's eyes clouded with worry for a moment. She recovered quickly and gave a short, decisive nod. "If God sent her to us, He has His reasons. Thief or no, Star has a good heart. I can see it in her eyes. And we'll do all we can for her. Let's start by getting her all snuggled in for the night. Oh, no." She clapped her hand to her cheek. "I forgot all about Aimee. Finish pouring the water and go tuck her in. She's missed you something awful."

Michael grinned as they went back inside. He'd missed her too. Steam rose up, clouding his vision as he poured the hot water into the tub. He only hoped God, and not a pretty face, had drawn him to Star. What if he had made a mistake bringing her into his home?

four

Star snuggled down between soft sheets and a quilt. Feeling remarkably cozy and warm, she closed her eyes and smiled. Michael's mother was wonderful, she decided. The woman had provided her with a hot bath, helped her dress, then tucked her into bed as though she were a child.

The memory of her own mama tucking her in for the night came back as a faraway image in the recesses of Star's mind, but it quickly became as vivid as though she were reliving the past. She could almost feel the gentle hands smoothing her hair back from her face, could almost hear Mama's whispered dreams of someday leaving Luke and buying a small home of their own. A place where Star could go to school and play with other children. Tears formed at the corners of Star's eyes.

Oh, Mama, I never cared where I lived or whether I had other children to play with. All I ever cared about was you. But you don't need to worry about me anymore. I got away from Luke. He'll never find me—not until I'm ready to face him for what he did to you.

A wrenching sob rose and became a groan as it left her lips. Her stomach tightened, and her body shook violently as the anguish she'd suppressed throughout the day now came pouring out. She pounded at the soft bed with her fists. *Why did he have to kill my mama?*

He wouldn't get away with it. Somehow, she would make Luke pay for what he'd done. When the time was right, she'd go back to Oregon City; and if Luke had already moved on, she'd track him down like the animal he was. He'd get what was coming to him. If it was the last thing she ever did on this earth, she'd make him pay.

A floorboard creaked, pulling Star from her vengeful thoughts. She stiffened. Suspicion clouded every sense. She knew it! Michael Riley was a snake if she'd ever seen one—and she'd seen plenty—enough to know what he was after. What sort of a man entered a woman's room when his own mother and daughter were in the next bed?

She balled up her fist and waited. If he so much as laid a fingernail on her, she'd scream and blacken his eye.

The muffled sounds of bare feet moved closer on the wooden planks. Star's heart hammered against her chest. Slowly, the covers on the opposite side of the bed lifted, letting in the cold. Star frowned as the bed moved a little. But not much. Even if he were particularly careful, Michael's weight would have made more of a dent in the mattress.

Opening one eye, Star ventured a peek. Recognizing the little intruder, she let out a relieved laugh. Aimee lay so close, they were practically nose to nose. Her wide brown eyes—so like her father's—stared curiously back at Star.

"What are you doing?" Star asked the little girl.

"Grammy's snoring real loud," Aimee whispered. "Can I sleep with you?"

"Well, what if I snore too?" Star teased.

The little girl seemed to consider the question. "Then I guess I'll go sleep in the barn with Cannonball." She let out a giggle. Star laughed at the joke, enchanted with the little pixie next to her. The child's face suddenly grew serious. "Miss Star?"

"Yes?"

"Did you come here to be my new mama?"

Star gasped. "Did your pa tell you that?"

"No."

A curious disappointment fluttered across Star's stomach. "No. I'm not going to be your new mama. Why do you ask?"

The little girl's face fell. "Because I don't got one. Most children do, you know. Only not me. Never had one. I keep praying and praying for God to send me a ma. I just thought maybe you were the one I prayed for."

Star knew she was no one's answer to prayer. She searched for comforting words to say, but could think of nothing suitable. She understood the pain of losing a mother, but at least she'd had seventeen years with hers. The poor child had never known a mother's love. "Well, if I was going to have a little girl, I couldn't think of a nicer one than you."

"I have an idea." Aimee's round eyes shone with the wonder of her brilliant plan.

"Tell me," Star said. But the child's next words nearly broke her heart.

"Let's pretend you're my mama. Just for tonight."

Star's breath left her lungs with a *whoosh*. "Oh, Aimee. I don't know if that's such a good idea." What would Michael think? He'd hit the roof if he thought she'd even entertained such a request.

Aimee's face clouded with disappointment. "Just until I fall asleep?"

"I've never been a mother, Sweetie. I wouldn't even know what to do. How about if we pretend I'm your aunt or your big sister, maybe?"

A scowl darkened the moonlit face. "Never mind." The frown lifted as soon as it had appeared and her expression brightened. "Could you tell me a story?"

Star's heart sank to her toes. She only knew a couple of stories, and they weren't even close to suitable for Michael's little girl, though she'd heard them when she was a child.

"I don't know any," she admitted.

"Not even one?"

Star shook her head. "I'm afraid not."

"But didn't your ma and pa ever tell you any stories?"

"I didn't have a pa," she replied, hoping Aimee wouldn't press that particular subject.

The little girl's eyes sobered with understanding. "Like I don't have a ma."

"Yes."

"Do you have a ma?"

"I used to, but she passed away."

Aimee reached out and touched Star's face with her soft hand. "Mine too."

Swallowing hard, Star fought back the tears threatening to begin all over again. She covered the pudgy little hand with one of her own, marveling at its sweet softness. "My mama had to work very hard to take care of me. She didn't have much time to tell me stories, but she tucked me in every night before she went to work."

Aimee sighed in obvious sympathy for Star's plight. "Grammy or Pa tucks me in, and they always tell me a story from the Bible. Want to hear one?"

Star made an effort to push away the sadness. "I'd love to hear a Bible story."

"Do you want one from the old part of the Bible or the new?"

"I thought the whole thing was pretty old."

A giggle escaped the tiny rosebud mouth. "You're funny."

She hadn't meant to be funny, but Star was glad her ignorance had brought the child some pleasure. Smiling, she brushed away a strand of golden hair from Aimee's cheek.

"I think you're pretty funny too. So what story do you want to tell me?"

Aimee scrunched her nose, her brow creasing as though she were deep in thought. "Well, there was a man named Jonah in the old part of the Bible. He was swallowed by a fish. Do you want to hear that one?"

Star felt her eyes grow wide as she pictured a catfish large enough to swallow a grown man. Rising up on her elbow, she rested her ear on her palm and nodded.

Aimee sat straight up.

"There was this man named Jonah," she began, then frowned. "I don't know any men named Jonah, do you?"

"I don't think so, but I've heard of lots of men named John."

"There's some of those in the Bible too. Want to hear about one of them?"

Star wanted to hear the fish story. "Let's finish the one about Jonah first."

"Oh, yeah." She grinned an infectious smile that Star couldn't help but return. "Well, God told Jonah to go to. . . to. . .Nin. . .Ninna. It was a town with very bad people who wouldn't obey God."

"Then why did God want to send Jonah there?" Star asked.

"I guess he was a traveling preacher, like the circuit riders that used to come around here until my uncle Hank started being the preacher regular-like."

"Oh. So God wanted Jonah to preach to the people in Ninna?"

"Yeah. Because they were really, really bad. Do you know what bad people do?"

"What?"

A shrug lifted the small shoulders. "Pa won't tell me. I just thought you might know."

Stifling a giggle, Star shook her head. After Michael's comments about her own conduct, she wasn't sure what "bad" was either. She had the feeling, the way Michael had pounced on the word she'd used earlier, it wouldn't bother him a bit to set her straight when the situation warranted. "Did Jonah go to Ninna like God told him to?"

Aimee's mop of curls bounced as she bobbed her head. "But not at first. He got in a boat with some men and went the other way."

"I wonder why he would do that." If God ever spoke to Star, she'd be so honored, it wouldn't bother her a bit to do exactly what she was told.

"Pa says he was a scaredy-cat."

"What was he afraid of?"

"I dunno. Maybe he thought he might get scalped. I guess it's like the preacher that tried to bring a little religion to the heathen redskins last year. They didn't want to hear it, so they scalped him."

"That's awful!"

"I heard Uncle Hank telling Pa about it awhile back. Pa said some folks would just rather live in their sin, and maybe it would be better to leave the Indians alone. Uncle Hank didn't think so, though."

Star wondered how Uncle Hank had heard about it, but even more, she wanted to get to the part of the story where Jonah got swallowed by the fish. "So what happened to Jonah after he got into the boat and went the other way?"

Aimee leaned forward, her eyes wide. "God sent a big storm." For emphasis, she held her arms out as far as they would go. "And the other men were real scared because the boat was tipping over and they didn't want to drown."

Star placed her palm flat on the bed. Pushing herself up higher, she rested her full weight on her hand. Her stomach tightened with the intensity of the story. "Did Jonah fall out of the boat? Is that how he got swallowed?"

"They threw him out! Wasn't that mean?"

It certainly was. "Why would they do such a thing?"

"I don't really understand why, but Jonah told them to do it. He knew if he got out of the boat, the storm would stop."

"What happened after they threw him in? The fish came and ate him?"

"Yep."

A twinge of regret snaked its way across Star's heart. "Then he died? I thought he went to Ninna to preach."

"He didn't die."

"He got swallowed up by a fish, but he didn't die?" Star couldn't keep the cynicism from her voice. Obviously, Aimee heard it, for she stiffened her spine and jutted her chin defensively. "Pa says that's the miracle part about it."

"Oh."

Aimee gave her a gap-toothed grin. "There's always a miracle in Bible stories. Jonah stayed in the fish for three whole days. I wouldn't want to do that, would you?"

"Huh-uh." Star shuddered at the thought.

"But Jonah prayed and told God he was sorry. And God made the fish swim over to the ground and throw him up. And Jonah was so glad to be out of the fish that he went to Ninna."

"I should hope so." Though it seemed to Star a preacher, of all people, should have known better than to disobey God in the first place.

"After he preached in Ninna, the folks there told God they were sorry for being bad, and God forgave them."

"Just like that? He didn't punish them?"

Aimee shook her head. "Pa says Jonah was kinda mad about that part. He thought God should punish the people."

"Well, that's probably because he had just spent three days in a fish's belly and wasn't feeling too happy about things in general."

"Probably," Aimee agreed, a wide yawn muffling the word. She lay back on the bed, so Star did the same. "But Uncle Hank says when a person is really sorry for the wrong things they do, that God throws the sin away just like it never happened."

"He does?"

"Yes, and if you ask Jesus to live in your heart, He makes you His child. And then you get to be with Him in heaven someday."

Tears stung Star's eyes. Aimee's eyes had drifted shut, but Star shook her. "Aimee, what else do you have to do to live with God in heaven someday?"

A soft sigh escaped the rosebud lips. "You have to tell God that you believe Jesus is His Son."

"I do believe that." *With all my heart.* "And then what?" she prodded. "Aimee, what next?"

Aimee's eyes popped open and she gave another wide yawn. "You have to believe Jesus died for your sins and then came back alive."

"I do." Joy rushed to her heart and burst forth. "I believe it, Aimee. I really do.

"What next?"

Her eyes closed once more and she snuggled under the covers. "That's it. Now you just have to be good."

"Oh, Sweetie. Thank you. Thank you so much."

"Mmmm. . ."

Star smiled and reached forward, caressing the child's golden curls. She would have loved to hear another story, but Aimee's steady breathing indicated she had already fallen asleep. Leaning forward carefully, she pressed a soft kiss to the child's forehead.

Rolling onto her back, Star folded her arms behind her head and stared up at the ceiling. The story amazed and perplexed her. On one hand, God let a fish swallow Jonah to punish him, but he forgave the wicked people in Ninna. Aimee had said when a person was sorry for what they did wrong, God threw the sin away. But what if a person didn't know what was right? What then? Star's eyes grew heavy and a yawn opened her mouth wide.

One thing she knew for sure, she had landed smack dab in the middle of a family who knew right from wrong, where folks read the Bible, and even a five year old could recount the stories by heart. If there was anyplace to find out about God, this was it. She could have done a lot worse.

With a sigh, she rolled back onto her side, trying to find a comfortable position in the unfamiliar bed. Her good foot bumped against the injured ankle. Instinctively, Star swore at the shooting pain. With a gasp, she covered her mouth and squeezed her eyes shut. "I'm sorry, God," she whispered. "I didn't mean to say it ever again."

She glanced at the little girl lying next to her and expelled a relieved breath. By the child's even breathing, Star knew she couldn't have heard the word.

Star groaned. She'd better learn to stop saying that before Michael took her straight back where he found her. Or worse, he might just throw her out and let her fend for herself. Then she'd never get a chance to find out everything he knew about God.

ૐ

Michael stripped off his jeans and cotton shirt and stretched out on his bed. The memory of his daughter's version of Jonah still lingered in his mind. He grinned into the darkness and shook his head. *Ninna.* He'd have to set Star straight tomorrow. When he heard Aimee's little voice in Star's bed, he had fully intended to order her back to his mother's bed. But when he heard her ask if Star wanted to hear about Jonah, he couldn't help but listen.

He couldn't figure Star out. One minute she was cussing as well as any drunken cowboy he'd ever heard; the next, she was listening with childlike wonder to one of the earliest Bible lessons taught in a Christian home. The puzzling part was that she seemed genuinely interested. When he heard her agree to the story, he'd assumed she only did it to appease Aimee. From the sound of it, she'd probably never picked up a Bible in her life. If she'd ever been to a church meeting, which he doubted, she apparently hadn't learned much. While she was under his roof, he'd have to do something about her lack of understanding on spiritual matters.

An owl called to its mate from the tall oak outside of Michael's loft window. He turned his head toward the sound. The light of the moon filtered in through the glass, casting a glow on the hope chest below the sill. Sarah's trunk. Michael had lovingly crafted it as a wedding gift for his wife. Painstakingly, he had carved out her initials in large script across the middle of the lid. On either side of the initials, facing inward, he had carved a dove, each carrying a leaf in its beak. Even now, Michael relived the disappointment he'd felt back then—that the symbolism for a new beginning was lost on Sarah.

She'd been genuinely happy with the beauty of the trunk but had been less than thrilled with the Bible accompanying the gift. Michael had never once seen her attempt to read it. He remembered her teasing laughter when he mentioned the oversight. "What do I need to read it for? You quote the Bible constantly. Folks could mistake you for a preacher or something."

He swallowed hard at the memory. He had met her while staying overnight in Portland, after driving a herd of cattle to sell. Sarah had worked in the saloon next to the hotel. He had met her on the street, a bruised, swollen lip marring her otherwise perfect face. Michael had taken her to a restaurant and bought her a meal and was desperately in love before the last bite was eaten. In a moment of unaccustomed impulsiveness, he had asked her to marry him. After all, hadn't she cried and told him how much she wanted to change? How much she wanted out of the life she led?

Throughout their three-day journey home, Sarah had listened to his talk of God. She had agreed with everything. She knew all about God, she'd said, but had gotten down on her luck and was forced into her sinful life just to make ends meet. Now she wanted to return to her roots and become respectable once again.

Michael's hand balled into a fist. He had been fooled, plain and simple. He should have known better, but his smitten heart had so wanted to believe her.

The memories strengthened his resolve to remove everything of Sarah's from his home. He knew Aimee would probably want the trunk when she grew up, so he kept it. Everything else would be burned. Except the Bible. Even in his anger, Michael knew he couldn't bring himself to destroy such a treasure.

A loud clatter drew him up straight in the bed, his heart pounding in his chest. What was that? He swung his legs around to the edge of the bed and grabbed his pants from the floor. Standing, he slipped on the jeans and buttoned them. He glanced at the Colt lying on the table next to his bed. After a moment's hesitation, he snatched up the gun. No telling what that noise could have been. Cannonball might have found a way inside, but the sound could have just as likely been caused by an outlaw up to no good.

Or it could be. . . *Don't let that pretty face fool you, Mister. That girl stole a load of cash from my boss and he wants it back.* . . .

Michael scowled as the words came back to haunt him. After he had saved her, brought her home, and let his daughter sleep in the same bed, Star was trying to rob him. Was there a woman alive, besides Ma, who could be trusted?

He looked down from the loft. A quick glance toward the bedroom confirmed the door was open. He inched down the ladder, ready to catch Star in the act. He wouldn't even wait until morning to take her into Hobbs and let the sheriff deal with her. He would be well rid of the little thief.

He stepped into the living area and, sure enough, there she was, stooped over by the cherry wood armoire his pa had built for Ma thirty years ago. Ma had insisted it was too beautiful to hide away in a bedroom, so the cupboard had always graced the main room of the house. It seemed only right that Ma bring it with her when she came to live with Michael after Aimee was born.

Anger boiled his blood at the thought of this girl going through his mother's things.

"What do you think you're doing?" he demanded, closing the distance between them in a few short strides.

Star gasped and spun around to face him. "Michael!"

He grabbed her by the arm. "Surprised?"

"Of course I'm surprised. Wouldn't you be if someone came sneaking up on you? I'm trying to find—"

In no mood to hear a pack of lies, Michael cut her off. "Save it for the sheriff."

"Michael Riley, turn that poor child loose."

Michael kept a firm grasp on Star's arm and faced his mother.

"Ma, I caught her red-handed trying to steal from us."

"N—no, I—"

"Don't be ridiculous," his mother snapped. "The girl wouldn't get past the barn with her injury. It took her ten minutes to get this far. And put down that gun. Have you taken leave of your senses?"

"Oh, Miss Hannah, I'm so sorry I woke you."

"Think nothing of it. Let me help you find whatever it is you were looking for."

Michael gaped at the two women, one contrite, eyes wide with fear; the other, his own mother, ready to help her loot the place.

"Ma—"

"You didn't even give her a chance to explain, so I don't want to hear anything you have to say. Shame on you for expecting the worst. Do as I said and let her go this instant."

Michael let go at once.

"Please don't argue on my account," Star begged.

Slapping his hand against his thigh, Michael glared at the girl. "Fine, tell me what you're doing skulking about the house at this time of night."

"I—I—"

Obviously, she was trying to think up a convincing lie. "Well? Make it good."

Her eyes narrowed, growing steely. He'd seen the same expression on her face just before she'd shoved him from the wagon during the storm. Instinctively, he stepped back.

"If you must know, I was looking for a candle so I could find my way to the privy! But I wasn't going to steal it, just borrow it."

Michael felt the anger drain from him.

Ma stepped between him and Star. "Let me help you outside, Honey. It's a good thing you made noise and woke me up. I doubt you'd have made it ten feet alone, anyway. Gracious, is that my teapot on the floor?"

"Yes, Ma'am. It fell off the cupboard and broke when I was trying to feel around for the candle. I'll find a way to pay you back for it. I promise."

"Nonsense. Accidents happen. Besides, it's as old as Adam. 'Bout time I bought another one."

Michael watched in bewilderment as his mother helped Star out the door. Guilt pricked him as he squatted down and started picking up the broken pieces. He knew for a fact how much his ma treasured that teapot. If he'd have been the one to break it, she'd have chewed him up one side and down the other; but for some reason, Ma had decided to become this girl's champion. There was nothing he could say or do to change her mind. When Ma got a notion in her head, that was that.

He disposed of the shattered teapot and returned to his loft. With a frustrated sigh, he sat on the edge of the bed and raked his fingers through his hair. The girl might be a heap of trouble and a heathen to boot, but there was nothing worse than being falsely accused. No doubt about it, he owed her an apology.

A grin lifted the corners of his mouth. He knew he could do better than an apology. Striding to the trunk, he lifted the lid. After rummaging through the clothing, he found Sarah's Bible. With a satisfied smile, he carefully closed the lid and walked into the bedroom. His little girl didn't stir as he bent and kissed her soft, round cheek and lifted the covers over her shoulders.

The front door opened as the women returned to the house. Quickly Michael set the gift on the table beside the bed and crept back to his loft, pleased with himself for fulfilling his duty. Not only to get that girl some religion, but he felt the gift equaled an apology. His assumption that she was stealing had been an honest mistake. Maybe Star wasn't stealing from them—this time, but she was *still* a thief. What else was he supposed to think with her sneaking around the house in the dead of night, looking through cupboards and such? He undressed for the third time that night and stretched out fully on the bed.

The glow of the lantern on the table made him smile. She'd see the Bible soon, and the light in her pretty eyes in the morning would be all the thanks he needed.

five

"It won't work, Michael Riley." Star plunked the Bible down on the table the next morning. She stumbled, trying to compensate for her injured ankle.

Michael's heart lurched as she nearly lost her balance. He reached out to steady her. Jerking away, she grabbed the edge of the table. Her knuckles grew white under the strain of holding her weight off the swollen ankle.

"What are you talking about?" he asked, stung by her reaction to his gift. He stood and grabbed a chair. "Sit down before you fall."

Red-faced and eyes blazing, she ignored him. "Only a low-down skunk would try to plant the Good Book in my room to make it look like I was trying to steal it!"

Ma set a plate of fluffy biscuits on the table. "Michael! How could you?"

"Now wait, you don't really think I—"

"Miss Star doesn't need a Bible, Pa. I'm telling her all about it, ain't I, Miss Star?"

In an instant, Star's expression softened. She turned to look at the little girl. "You sure are. I loved the story you told me last night. If I'm still around tonight, maybe you could tell me another one."

"You're not going anywhere, are you?" Aimee's soft brows drew together.

"That depends on. . ." Star turned her steely gaze back to Michael. "Well, that just depends."

"Pa, don't send her away!"

"Now look, you've gone and made the child cry." Ma gathered Aimee in her arms. "Of course Star isn't going anywhere, sweet thing."

"Hang on a minute, all of you." Still holding the chair he had offered Star, Michael lifted it a good two inches off the floor and let it clatter back down for emphasis.

"Sit," he ordered, this time taking her firmly by the arm. "You need to stay off that if it's ever going to heal."

Surprisingly, she obeyed.

Taking the chair at the end of the table, he set it next to her and turned her around. "Prop your foot up." Once she was situated, Michael sat back in his own chair. "I didn't plant that Bible to try to trap Star into stealing it." He looked from his mother to Aimee, then rested his gaze on Star. "It was meant as a gift."

Her lips parted as she drew in a quick breath.

Forcing himself not to stare at the softness of her mouth, he met her wide-eyed gaze. "My way of apologizing for accusing you of stealing last night."

"You were giving it to me?"

"I *am* giving it to you." Michael slid the black book across the table to her. "It's yours if you want it."

"Hmmph. . .seems to me you were trying to bribe your way out of a real apology," Ma said.

Star grabbed up the Bible and hugged it to her chest like a dog hoarding a bone. "Oh, no. This is fine. I accept. No harm done."

Ma's face softened as her gaze rested on the girl. Lowering her plump form into a chair, she glanced up at Michael and gave him an approving smile. "Sit down and say the blessing, Son."

A warm glow enveloped Michael at the almost tangible excitement on Star's face. Only when Ma insisted she eat, did the girl release her death grip on the Bible, setting it reverently next to her plate.

Why couldn't Sarah have felt that way about it? he thought pensively. He berated himself. He had to stop comparing Star to Sarah. But it was only natural, he reasoned. They were exactly the same sort—women of loose morals and questionable character. Was there really a difference between a thief and a prostitute? Not according to the Bible. Sin was sin. Of course, he had to admit, Star's reaction to his gift gave him some hope that she, at least, was redeemable.

"Michael?" Ma's voice drifted through his bitter thoughts. "Did you hear what I said?"

"Sorry, Ma," he muttered. "My mind was somewhere else."

Ma released an exasperated breath. "I *said*, the new teacher's due to arrive in a month or so."

Michael looked up sharply. "Hank found a teacher?"

"Just got the letter last week. A woman from Kansas."

"Well, that's good news."

"Can I go to school?" Aimee nearly bounced in her chair.

"Sit still," Michael scolded, softening his words with a smile. The little girl's face clouded over, but she obeyed. "Well, can I?"

"We'll just have to wait and see."

She let out a sigh and turned toward Star. "Wait and see usually means no. But I don't see why I can't go."

Star grinned. "I think your pa just means he's not sure how old you have to be to attend school."

"I'll be six pretty soon. And I already know my ABC's. I can even read if the words are little."

Star's smile fairly lit the room as she beamed at the child. "Already? You know what? I'd bet my last penny that by the time school starts, you'll be old enough. Right, Michael?" Reaching out, Star smoothed Aimee's curls. The maternal gesture took Michael by surprise, and so did his pleasant reaction. But he knew better than to allow Aimee to grow too attached to their temporary houseguest. He'd have to discuss the matter with Star. Soon. Very soon.

"Michael?"

"Pa!"

Michael blinked and stared from one to the other. "What? Oh, yeah. Probably." He hated the thought of his little girl going off to school. How was it possible she was even old enough?

Tossing his napkin down on his empty plate, he stood. "Ma, I'm going into Hobbs. Need anything?"

"Nothing I can think of. What are you going to town for? You brought plenty of supplies from Oregon City."

Michael shrugged. "Just need a few more things."

"Can I go, Pa?" Aimee shot from her chair and ran to grab Michael's hand.

"*May* I go," Ma corrected.

Aimee glanced at Ma, then back up at Michael. "Grammy wants to go too."

Ma shook her head and gave him a helpless smile. "I think she'd better get some schooling soon before there's no hope for her."

Swinging the little girl up in his arms, Michael cast a glance at his mother. "Have any plans for her today? I wouldn't mind taking her with me." While he hated to indulge his daughter too much, he'd missed the little tyke and they'd always made these short trips to town together.

With a wave of her hand, Ma dismissed them both and set about cleaning up the plates. "Go on and take her. If you don't, she'll just pout and be underfoot until you get back."

Michael set her down and gave her little rump an affectionate swat. "Go get your jacket. There's a chill in the air this morning."

"A'right, Pa," she returned, happily running to do as she was told. She grabbed her jacket from its hook by the door and shrugged it on. After buttoning her up, Michael offered his hand.

Aimee hung back, turning to Star. "You going to be here when I get back?"

"I promise." Star smiled with affection.

A grin tipped the child's lips. "Mrs. Merlin always gives me a sourball when we go to the mercantile. I'm going to ask for one for you too. Let's go, Pa." Tugging on his hand, she led the way out the door.

ঽ

Mrs. Merlin's eyebrows rose in obvious curiosity when Michael asked to see dress goods. "Your ma feeling too poorly to come pick out her own material these days?"

Michael shook his head. "Ma's feeling right as rain. Thank you for asking, Ma'am."

The older woman sniffed and pulled down two bolts of fabric—one, the ugliest brown muslin Michael had ever seen—the other, a gray piece he could only describe as matronly. Neither would do for a young woman with Star's creamy complexion and violet eyes. But how did he go about explaining that to the proprietress without giving her more information than she needed to know—information sure to be all over Hobbs before his wagon rolled out of town?

Aimee saved him the trouble, making Michael sorry he'd ever brought her along. "Oh, it's not for Grammy. It's for Miss Star. She don't have any clothes, and Pa don't want her wearing my ma's old things."

A pleased smile lit Mrs. Merlin's pinched face at the easily obtained morsel of information. "I see. And who is Miss Star?"

Indignation hit Michael square in the gut. The woman didn't even have the grace to direct the question to him!

"Pa brought her back with him from Oregon City," Aimee said matter-of-factly, her pink tongue sliding over her lips as she eyed a jar of sourballs on the counter.

With an elated smirk, the shameless woman twisted off the lid and offered the jar to the little girl. "Take one, and tell me about Miss Star."

Feeling his collar tighten like a noose around his neck, Michael reached up and loosened his top button.

"Miss Star is beyoootiful!" Aimee began enthusiastically, ready to tell everything she knew and then some. "When Pa carried her inside last night, I thought she was going to be my new m—"

Michael recovered enough to slip his arm around the back of his little girl's head and cup his hand over her mouth in the nick of time.

"He carried her inside?" Giving him a triumphant smile, Mrs. Merlin cocked an eyebrow and waited. Michael would have liked nothing better than to give her a sound piece of his mind but, aware of his daughter's presence, swallowed the words past a boulder-sized lump in his throat.

Resigned, he expelled a long, slow breath and relented. "The girl will be staying on to help out around the place. Ma's not as pert as she used to be and could use someone to take over part of the chores."

Mrs. Merlin continued to stare, a look of impatience on her face. "You carried her inside?"

"She had a little accident and couldn't walk," Michael said firmly. "And that's all there is to it."

The woman scowled, obviously not getting all the information she wanted. She let out a huff and turned her attention back to the bolts of fabric on the counter. " 'Bout how much of this do you want?"

Michael fingered the brown muslin, scanning the shelves until his gaze rested on a bolt of deep green muslin. *Pretty enough for a girl like Star.* Dropping the drab brown muslin, he pointed at the shelf. "Actually, I was thinking more of something like that—enough for a dress." He cleared his throat. "And some of that blue over there."

"Kinda fancy for hired help, I'd say."

"The girl has to have something to wear to church," he said, defenses raised.

"If you say so," she shot back, with a shrug that clearly indicated she had her own opinion.

Michael left the store a few moments later, carrying a bundle containing enough material for four dresses—one blue, the closest color he found to match Star's eyes; the green, because it was his favorite color; and the brown and gray, because Mrs. Merlin seemed to think they were more fitting than the material he had chosen. In no mood to argue, Michael had bought the whole bundle. At the woman's suggestion, he'd also plunked down money for material to make underclothes. He'd had to guess on the size for a pair of sturdy boots; but by the time he'd gotten that far, Michael was so fed up with Mrs. Merlin's questions and hints, he didn't care if they pinched Star's toes into tight balls or if they swallowed her feet whole. He just had to get out of that store before the busybody drove him crazy.

On the way home, Aimee chattered incessantly until her eyes drooped and she fell asleep against his arm. When he reached the homestead, Michael lifted her gently from the wagon seat and carried her up to the house. He stopped at the sound of a deep, booming laugh that could only belong to one person. He groaned inwardly. Andy had returned.

❧

Star's heart did a funny little flip-flop when Michael walked inside carrying Aimee in his arms. He stood tall in the doorway, staring at his brother, a scowl on his face.

Not fifteen minutes after Michael's wagon had rolled out of sight, his brother burst through the door, grabbed up Miss Hannah, and swung her around the room. Thinking he was an intruder, Star had grabbed a broom and would have whopped him a good one, if not for the look of pure joy on the older woman's face.

"Michael!" Andy's voice resonated throughout the house. "Good to see you."

Michael's scowl deepened as Aimee stirred and lifted her sleepy head. Her mouth popped open as she stared at Andy.

Star couldn't blame her for staring. The man stood well over six feet tall. His hair, the same reddish-brown color as Michael's, hung shoulder length in almost feminine waves. But there wasn't a thing feminine about the rest of him. Broad shoulders and a thick chest filled out his buckskin shirt and, with a bushy beard covering his face, he looked downright scary.

"Pa? Who's that?"

"Who am I?" Andy said. "I'm your uncle Andy, little girl. And I have a present for you."

"You do?" Aimee wiggled until Michael set her on the floor. She walked toward her uncle, eyeing him cautiously.

"I sure do. Traded a fine pouch of tobacco to a little Indian squaw to get it."

Star glanced at Michael. He definitely was not happy to see this brother. Curiosity piqued, Star wondered if they'd had a falling out or if Michael just didn't like people in general.

"Pa says tobacco's evil."

A grin spread across Andy's face. "That a fact?"

"Yes." Aimee wrinkled her nose. "And it's nasty too. All that spittin' and stuff."

Andy threw back his head and let out a belly laugh that fairly shook the house. "Good thing I got rid of it, then, isn't it?"

He riffled through his saddlebags and pulled out an Indian doll. She wore a fringed buckskin dress and a beaded band around her straw head.

Aimee stared wide-eyed. "Is that for me?" she whispered.

"Sure is. You're not too grown up to play with dolls, are you?"

"No, Sir." She reached out her pudgy hands.

"Where are your manners, young lady?" Miss Hannah asked.

"Thank you, Uncle Andy." She hugged the doll tightly to her chest, then gave him a puzzled frown. "How come you're my uncle? I only had Uncle Hank before."

That seemed to draw Michael out of whatever state he was in. He stepped forward and extended his hand to his brother.

Star breathed a relieved sigh when Andy clasped the proffered hand and grinned. Michael seemed to relax. There was obviously trouble between the two men.

"Uncle Andy is your uncle because he's my other brother," Michael explained to the little girl. "And he's been gone since right after you were born." His voice held the disapproval Star was learning to dread, but it didn't seem to bother Andy in the least. As a matter of fact, he let the challenge go and focused on his niece.

"That's a fact," Andy said with a nod. He grinned and reached forward to tweak Aimee's nose. " 'Course, back then, you were a wrinkly, squalling little thing and not nearly so pretty as you are now. You were just about as big as that doll, I'd say. Maybe a little bigger."

At the reminder of her gift, the little girl turned suddenly to Michael. "Where's the presents we brought for Star, Pa?"

Presents? For her?

Star glanced up into Michael's flushed face. He cleared his throat. "I bought a few things to get Star through the winter," he explained, the red on his face deepening and creeping up to his ears.

"I'll go get it." Aimee bounded from the house before anyone could say a word.

Star glanced down at the ill-fitting, pink satin dress she wore, one Michael had grudgingly allowed her to borrow from his wife's trunk. He must have loved the woman very much to have kept her things all these years. Star could only imagine how painful it must be for him to see another woman wearing them.

Truth be told, the gown wasn't exactly comfortable for Star either. She'd never worn such a tight, low-cut dress before—nor satin. Ma had always insisted upon her wearing modest, high-necked, dark dresses revealing the least amount of her curves. Though Star had longed for the pretty things at the time, now she understood Ma was keeping her hidden to protect her.

An all-too-familiar ache swelled inside her heart. How she missed Ma. She struggled to push the pain aside. Lila had said there was a time for grieving, but now wasn't the time. Only in solitude could she relieve her sorrow through tears.

Aimee returned to the house carrying a fat bundle in her little arms. She shoved it at Star and bounded back toward the door. "I'll get the other one," she threw over her shoulder.

The other one? How long would it take for her to pay for this and start saving her money?

She turned to Michael. Looking everywhere but at her, he shifted his position and cleared his throat again. "Well, I best get to the chores. Looks like more rain is coming in soon."

With that, he headed for the door, practically knocking Aimee over in the process.

" 'Cuse me, Pa," the little girl said, as he grabbed onto her to keep her from tumbling to the floor. Michael bent to give her a quick kiss on the head and was gone in a flash.

Aimee handed Star another fat bundle. "You'll like what Pa picked out." She scrunched up her nose. "Mrs. Merlin made him buy some ugly colors too, but Pa says you can do chores in those and wear the pretty dresses to church and town and such."

"Your pa bought me dresses?"

" 'Course not. We don't have ready-made dresses in town. Mrs. Merlin don't think it's prof. . .prof. . ." Her brow furrowed as she tried to think of the word. Then she gave up with a shrug. "She don't think anyone would buy them."

Miss Hannah grinned. "Mrs. Merlin doesn't think it's profitable to have ready-made gowns in the store."

"Then what do you mean, I can wear them to church and for chores?"

"Pa got some pretty material for you to make you dresses. When are you going to start?"

Star's stomach turned over, and she thought she might fall off the chair. How could she ever bring herself to tell Michael she didn't know how to sew?

She glanced at Miss Hannah. The older woman gave her an encouraging smile. "It's all right. Michael wouldn't have bought the things if he didn't think you needed them."

Wishing the woman had read her mind, Star felt her heart sink. She was just going to have to find a way to explain that she couldn't make the dresses. Sarah's gowns would have to do for her.

"I don't see anything wrong with what she's wearing now." Andy gave her a once-over and winked.

Feeling her face grow hot under his appreciative gaze, Star looked away uncomfortably. She'd seen that look before on the faces of dozens of other men, and she'd just as soon never see it again.

Miss Hannah stood. "You'll be wanting to take these things to your room so you can rummage through them. Let me help you in there."

"Want me to carry her, Ma?"

"No!" Star said, a little too sharply.

His brow lifted. "Just trying to be helpful," he said with a smirk.

"Thank you, but I–I can make it. Really. It's not hurting nearly as bad as it was before."

Miss Hannah slid an arm around Star's shoulders. "Lean on me, Honey. Aimee, carry Miss Star's new things into our room, will you?"

Star drew in a sharp breath as she tried to step down on her swollen ankle.

Andy stepped forward. "Sure you don't want me to—"

"No!" Star and Miss Hannah said in unison.

He held his palms up in surrender. "Okay, okay, just trying to be a gentleman."

Throwing him a reproving look, Miss Hannah gave a disgruntled sniff. "Behave yourself, young man, before I turn you over my knee and whip the daylights out of you."

Andy chortled. "Aw, Ma."

"Don't 'Aw, Ma' me," she shot back, but her voice had softened considerably. "You just stay put until I get back. No telling how long 'til you up and take off again, and I haven't got my fill of you yet."

"Yes, Ma'am," he replied, that big grin plastered on his rugged face.

Star was glad when they reached the safety of her bedroom. That man made her uncomfortable.

As if reading her thoughts, Miss Hannah gave her shoulders a squeeze. "Don't worry about Andy, Honey. He's just a big young-un at heart. He don't mean anything he says."

"Yes, Ma'am." But Star couldn't shed the uneasiness filling her. She'd seen enough big, good-looking men with funny ways sweep the girls right off their feet, only to leave the next morning, never to be heard from again. She didn't care for his kind, and she didn't like the way he looked at her—as though he had a right. Michael never made her feel uncomfortable or undressed in the way his eyes held their own appreciation for her looks.

Aimee dumped the first bundle on the bed. "I'll get the other one," she hollered and ran out the door.

"Well, you going to open these packages and see what my son brought you?" Miss Hannah eyed her.

Star couldn't help but feel the excitement of getting the new things, although they would do her no good unless no one minded if she wrapped the material around her like a shawl. She smiled at the thought of Michael's face, should she do just that.

"You're a lovely girl, Star. Especially when you smile."

Surprised at the sudden compliment, she didn't know what to say as she glanced up to meet the older woman's gaze.

Cupping Star's cheeks in her work-roughened hands, Miss Hannah seemed to see straight through to her very soul. "You're a good girl, Honey. I don't know what trouble brought you to us, but I'm mighty thankful the Lord saw fit to bring Michael across your path."

Removing her hands, she let out a sigh and dropped to the bed beside Star. "We all have our share of troubles to muddle through. Sometimes we need to work things out for ourselves; but if the time comes when you feel the need to unburden yourself, you can come to me."

Again, Star was left speechless. Her throat tightened and her eyes stung. She kept her gaze directed to the packages spread out over the bed.

"Well, I'll leave you to open these by yourself," Miss Hannah said. She placed her hands on her thighs to brace herself and stood. "You feel free to use my sewing kit to fix yourself those dresses. Won't be able to do much else for the next week or so, with that ankle looking big enough to choke a horse."

Star lifted her hands in despair. Gathering her courage, she faced the woman. "Miss Hannah. . .I can't. I mean, I don't know how to. . ."

A puzzled frown furrowed the woman's brow, then changed to an understanding smile. "Why, you can't sew a stitch, can you?"

Dropping her gaze, Star shook her head.

"Well, there's nothing to it. Trust me, we'll whip them up in no time. By the time that ankle allows you to go to church, you'll be lovely as a picture in one of those pretty colors."

Church. Star's stomach nearly leapt with the joyous thought. She willed her ankle to hurry up and heal.

six

Three weeks later, Star swirled around the main room of the homestead while Miss Hannah and Aimee watched with delight. The wide skirt of her newly made green muslin dress brushed against Aimee, nearly knocking her off her feet.

Laughing aloud, Star snatched up the little girl and danced her around the room. "Oh! Have you ever seen anything so pretty in your life?"

A giggling Aimee shook her head.

"Your grammy's a sewing genius!"

Breathless, Star plopped down in the wooden rocker near the fireplace. Unable to contain the emotions welling up inside, she hugged Aimee tightly until the little girl began to squirm.

Miss Hannah beamed under the praise. "Oh, now. You'll be sewing your own dresses in no time."

"You really think so?"

"Why, sure. Nothin' to it. Right after dinner, we'll start cuttin' out the gray material."

Aimee turned her pixie face to Star and wrinkled her nose. "I don't like the gray. Do you?"

Star pressed her lips together. She couldn't very well admit to thinking that material was about as ugly as the brown dress Miss Hannah had already made.

"Can't Miss Star make the blue dress first? Then she could wear it to church on Sunday."

Star glanced hopefully at Miss Hannah.

The older woman shook her head. "I think it best we let Miss Star learn on the gray material. What do you think, Star?"

Swallowing her disappointment, she nodded. She detested

70

the gray, but Miss Hannah was right. No sense making a mess out of the pretty material.

Besides, now that her ankle was healed, she would begin all the outside chores in the morning. It had just about healed, and she'd tried to be too independent. As a result, she set back her healing and earned a thorough scolding from Michael. She already had the ugly brown muslin, but since there were more "every" days than special days, it was only practical to have two dresses to wear around the house.

A low whistle brought Star back to the present.

"You look as fresh and pretty as a summer forest." Andy's large buckskin-clad frame filled the door. His gaze raked over Star, making her feel undressed.

"Thank you," she mumbled, feeling the heat rush to her cheeks. Oh, what she wouldn't give for one chance to put that scoundrel in his place. But her mind went blank, and her hands started shaking every time he made an ungentlemanly or improper remark. The words she would like to say fled her mind, only to resurface at some later moment when she was alone with her thoughts. That did her no good at times like this.

"The dress is lovely, Star. You look very nice."

At the sound of Michael's voice, Star glanced up and smiled. "Thank you." The look of appreciation in his eyes thrilled her, reducing Andy's unwanted attention to a mere annoyance rather than a cause for concern.

"Is it already dinnertime?" Miss Hannah pushed herself up from her chair. "You boys sit yourselves down. I'll have your meal on the table in no time."

"I'll help." Star followed Miss Hannah to the stove, wishing she didn't have to walk past Andy to get there. She recoiled as he leaned in close enough to brush against her.

"Mmm, smell good too."

Star sent him her best look of disdain. She was getting pretty tired of his comments. Over the past three weeks, he seemed to have gotten steadily worse—finding opportunities to brush against her, making comments that weren't at all fitting or proper. To Star, it was as though she were back at Luke's and putting up with leers and suggestions from the drunken patrons. She avoided contact with him as best she could and prayed he'd feel the call of the wild and be on his way soon.

"Leave her alone, Andy," she heard Michael growl.

"Jealous?" Andy's mocking voice shot back.

Holding her breath, Star waited for the answer.

"Of course I'm not jealous. But common sense can tell you she doesn't appreciate your so-called admiration, so why keep baiting her like that?"

Andy gave an unpleasant chuckle. "I think she does appreciate the attention."

"Andy. . . ," Michael growled.

"Now, come on. What do you really know about this girl? You picked her up off the street without even asking around about her. No telling where she came from." He gave a short laugh. "And unless I miss my guess, she's closer to my kind of woman than yours."

Star felt the heat rise to her cheeks and tears burned her throat. Was it that obvious where she had come from? A sense of helpless fury invaded her. How would she ever gain respect if one look at her convinced people she was no good? She would just have to do something about her looks—that was all.

Michael's sharp response drew her from her thoughts of a pinched hairdo and drab gowns.

"If you don't shut your mouth, I'm going to shut it for you."

A gasp escaped Star's lips. "Oh, no! They can't fight. Miss Hannah, do something."

"I'm putting a stop to this nonsense." Miss Hannah scowled and grabbed the broom from the corner as Andy and Michael slammed to the floor, a tangle of long arms and legs. "You boys stop it this instant," Miss Hannah bellowed, raising the broom up high and bringing it down hard on Andy's leg.

"Ow, Ma! Will you move away before you get hurt?"

"I will not. You two don't have any sense at all," she huffed. "You're acting like a couple of young'uns."

From the corner, a meek voice piped up. "I don't hit people, Grammy. And I'm a young'un."

Star's gaze flew to Aimee's wide-eyed stare and trembling lips. The sheltered child looked as though she would dissolve into tears any second. The weight of responsibility for being the cause of Aimee's pain pressed into Star's chest. She gathered a deep, unsteady breath.

"Michael," she pleaded. "Please don't fight to defend me. I'm not worth it."

The two men stopped midstruggle, and all eyes turned to Star. She swallowed hard, trying to choke back the tears. "Please. . .just stop."

Miss Hannah's heavy arm pulled Star close. "You're worth every punch, darling Star. But these boys know fightin' don't solve a thing." She glared at Michael and Andy. "Now, get up off that floor, both of you. You two weren't raised to settle your differences with your fists. Andy, keep your mouth shut about Star from now on. She's a decent, God-fearing child, and I will not stand for any more of your disrespect."

Andy rose to his feet and offered his hand to Michael. Star held her breath as he pulled Michael to his feet.

Bending down, Michael pressed a kiss to Miss Hannah's anger-flushed cheek. "I'm sorry, Ma. No more fighting."

"Glad to hear it, Son. Now what about you?" She pointed the question to Andy.

Following Michael's example, he kissed his mother. "I reckon it's time for me to be pushin' on, anyway."

"Oh, Andy," Miss Hannah moaned. "Ya don't have to leave. I just want you to behave yourself like a gentleman."

"Now, Ma, it's not just because of this scuffle. You know I can't stay put for long. To tell you the truth, I'm headed East to scout for a wagon train, come spring."

"Andy, please," Star heard herself say, "I should be the one to leave. It will break your ma's heart if you go."

Giving her a lopsided grin, Andy bent at the waist in an exaggerated bow. "That's generous of you, *Miss* Star, but it's time for me to go. Although, I'll sure miss the sight of your pretty face."

"Listen, Andy," Michael said, his voice conciliatory, "I'd like you to stay. I could use your help with the harvest and, as Star said, Ma's going to miss you something awful if you leave again."

Andy hesitated, then shook his head. "I'm not much good in the fields."

"Pa?" Aimee's uncharacteristically meek voice captured their attention. "Is everything okay now?"

Michael lifted her from the floor and held her close. "Pa's sorry for scaring you, Angel. Everything's fine and dandy."

"No more fighting?"

"Nope," Andy cut in. "Your pa and I made up like a couple of lovebirds. And your uncle Andy is ashamed as all get out to scare you like that. Forgive me?"

A grin split Aimee's precious face as she bobbed her head, allowing her golden curls to bounce on her shoulders. "They got any Indian squaws where you're goin'?"

"Probably." Andy chuckled and sent her a wink. "Got any particular reason for asking, or were you just wondering?"

"You think you could bring me another Indian dolly?"

"Aimee!" Miss Hannah scolded.

Michael scowled at his daughter.

Throwing back his head, Andy, emitting a belly laugh, grabbed the little girl from Michael's arms and lifted her high into the air. "You bet I will. You just wait. I'll find the prettiest Indian doll I can find and bring it all the way back here just for you."

Miss Hannah gathered a deep, unsteady breath. "Well, no need to leave on an empty stomach. You sit yourself down, and I'll bring your dinner in a jiffy."

Star's heart clenched as she watched the older woman lift her apron and swipe at her eyes. She would have appealed to Andy once more, but as she turned to face him, she found his steely gaze boring into her, all but daring her to speak.

Fear shot through her, and her knees threatened to give way. Eager to escape, she followed Miss Hannah to the kitchen area.

❧

Michael stood in the predawn darkness and watched as Andy mounted his black mare.

"I sure wish you'd reconsider leaving, Andy," he said, surprised to find he really meant the words. After a lot of prayer and soul searching, he'd repented of his attitude toward his brother and for the brawl.

"Thanks anyway, little brother," Andy said with an easy grin. "But I think we both know this is for the best. But you be careful with that girl. Something don't quite add up about her, and I have a feeling you might know what it is. I just hope you know what you're doing."

"I do," Michael replied tersely.

"Maybe you do, and maybe you don't." Andy's shoulders lifted in a shrug. "Anyway, it's none of my business. I'll be seeing you when the wagon train makes it back to Oregon next year. I hope that woman doesn't do the same number on you Sarah did."

"Let me worry about that." Michael lifted a hand in farewell. Irritation threatened to rise again as he watched his brother ride away.

Maybe he was a little jealous of Andy's easy way with women, of the way he seemed to understand certain types. Andy had been right about Star. She was a questionable woman, though he'd never admit it to his brother in a million years. The girl was trying, after all, and she deserved to be given a chance. It had been a couple of weeks since he'd heard one undesirable word leave her lips, and each night he'd seen the glow of her candle at the table as she read her Bible. Each morning when he asked her about the previous night's text, her face lit like the midday sun, and she enthusiastically recounted what she'd read. Yes, Star was trying. He had to give her credit for that. She had proven herself beyond his expectations. Her growth spiritually was nothing short of miraculous. Even Ma had commented on that fact.

And now that Star's ankle was completely healed, he greatly anticipated escorting her to church in the morning.

seven

Star felt the warmth of contentment envelop her, despite the chill in the Sunday morning air. Seated in the back of the wagon with Aimee, she was hard-pressed to contain her excitement at the thought of her first church meeting ever.

The little girl's lively descriptions of the people and town had her giggling like a child.

Apparently, Mrs. Merlin knew everything about everybody and used her mercantile as a lively gossip shop, so Star should be careful what she said when that woman was anywhere close by. Least that's what Grammy said—more than once, according to Aimee.

Old Mr. Cooper never made it past the singing before he nodded off. Uncle Hank had too many manners to holler at him and wake him up, though Grammy thought it would teach the old man a fine lesson if Uncle Hank did. The snoring was downright distracting, and someone should really do something about it.

Star sat mesmerized as Aimee's descriptions of the townsfolk painted vivid pictures in her mind. The beautiful new seamstress had only been in town for a few months, it seemed. Everyone thought she must be hiding a "teeerrrible" secret for a woman that pretty to be living alone and running her own business. According to Mrs. Merlin, the woman was making herself mannish and needed to find a good husband to take care of her. But Grammy said Miss Rosemary was a smart young woman, looking after her own interests.

"Honestly, Aimee," Miss Hannah huffed from the wagon seat. "Talk about something else."

Aimee gave Star a bewildered look, then shrugged. "I'll tell you all about the Simpson twins later," she whispered. "Mrs.

Merlin says they need to find husbands too, but they're getting a little long in the tooth so the pickin's are getting mighty slim."

Star laughed out loud, gaining her a questioning glance from Miss Hannah. "Tell me about the church service," she suggested to divert the child's attention and hopefully keep them both out of trouble.

"First we all stand up and say the Lord's Prayer," Aimee said, her eyes brightening at the fresh topic. "I know it by heart. Want to hear me say it?"

"I'd love it," Star answered, not sure what the Lord's Prayer was.

"Our Father, which art in Heaven, hallow be thy name."

The little girl's nose scrunched and a frown furrowed her brow. "I wonder why the Lord called his father Hallow, don't you? Everyone knows God's name is God, and why didn't Jesus just call Him Pa, since He's His son?"

"I don't know."

"The word's *hallowed*, Aimee," Michael's deep voice said with a chuckle from the wagon seat. "It means holy."

"Oh." Apparently satisfied with the answer, Aimee turned her attention back to Star. "Ain't my pa smart about Bible stuff?"

Star couldn't deny it. Michael had become quite the teacher in the last few weeks, explaining Scriptures she didn't understand.

"*Isn't* your pa smart," Miss Hannah corrected from her seat next to Michael.

"That's just what I was saying to Miss Star, Grammy. Pa sure is smart."

Miss Hannah shook her head. "I give up."

The rest of the trip to town was filled with laughter, and Star felt positively lighthearted until the wagon approached the white church and rolled to a stop.

Aimee hopped down and raced to join a small girl who was just climbing from her own wagon.

"Walk!" Miss Hannah called as Michael helped her down. "That child will be the death of me yet."

With a shaky breath, Star watched Miss Hannah walk toward the building. She knew she should hop down and follow, but nerves held her fast.

Wagons lined the small churchyard; and men, women, and children filed into the church, dressed in their Sunday best.

Star's stomach suddenly began to churn at the memory of folks, much like these, who turned away from her on the streets of Oregon City. Would she receive the same welcome here?

"Coming, Star?"

Michael's throaty voice brought her about to face him. Heat rushed to her cheeks as she accepted the hand he held out for her. "Sorry," she muttered, her stomach doing flip-flops from the gentle warmth of his touch.

"Don't worry," he murmured, leaning in close enough that his breath fanned her cheek. "You'll fit right in."

"I—I'm not worried." Star lifted her chin to emphasize her point.

A low chuckle rumbled from Michael's chest. "You ought to check out the Ten Commandments," he whispered, holding out his arm. "There's one there about lying."

Slipping her trembling hand through his arm, Star smiled in spite of herself. "Maybe I am a little nervous. One look at me, and everyone will know I'm different."

"You're right about that."

Taken aback, Star stopped midstep, jerking Michael's arm as she did so. "Is it really that obvious that I'm not like these folks?" she whispered, ready to turn around and run all the way back to the farm.

"Yep." Michael's brown eyes twinkled down at her. "If any of those girls had your beautiful eyes and curls as rich as molasses, they wouldn't be caught dead wearing that gray dress. And I noticed you pulled your hair back so tight, your eyes look like you'd have a hard time blinking."

So she looked plain. That's exactly what she had hoped to accomplish, wasn't it? But somehow, seeing herself through

Michael's eyes brought her no pleasure whatsoever. As a matter of fact, she had the urge to yank the knot from her hair and let her curls frame her face. But Michael's next words brought her back to her objective.

"You look very respectable." He looked at her kindly, all traces of teasing gone from his handsome face. "And not one person in that church will have a reason to think otherwise."

"You really think so?"

Holding out his arm once more, Michael nodded. "I know so—unless, of course, the singing starts without us. It wouldn't do for the preacher's brother to walk in late with a pretty girl on his arm. That would set tongues wagging for sure."

Star grabbed his arm and fairly dragged Michael toward the church doors. "Hurry up, then," she insisted, filing away the "pretty girl" comment for another time when she could be alone with her thoughts and remember the pleasure of the compliment upon Michael's lips.

The fresh smell of newly cut pine filled Star's senses as she stepped into the church with Michael at her side. The room, which had hummed when they walked in, suddenly grew silent as people stopped to stare.

Dropping her gaze to the plank floor, Star took an instinctive step closer to Michael.

To keep her gaze averted among decent folks was a habit born of years of receiving haughty glances, looks she'd rather die than have to bear—especially today, when all she wanted to do was attend the church meeting, just like she belonged.

She didn't want to give Mrs. Merlin anything too juicy to share with her customers at the mercantile the following day.

Feeling the pressure of Michael's hand at her elbow, Star glanced up. He inclined his head toward a bench at the front of the church where Aimee and Miss Hannah were already seated.

Star swallowed hard, a sense of dread pressing on her already nervous stomach. She was going to have to walk all the way up there?

Michael dipped his head and spoke close to her ear. "We'll be there before you know it. Move one foot after the other."

Spurred on by his sympathetic tone, Star did as he bade. She made haste, keeping her gaze fixed on her destination. Once there, she quickly sat next to Aimee.

Michael took his seat at the end of the bench, next to Miss Hannah. Disappointment flitted across Star's heart. She had rather looked forward to sitting next to him. The disappointment was short-lived, however, as Aimee slipped her warm hand inside Star's, sending an overwhelming sense of contentment through her.

"That's Uncle Hank," the little girl whispered, pointing to the man striding to the pulpit centered at the front of the church. Unlike Andy, Hank's looks weren't too similar to Michael's. His hair wasn't the reddish-brown she admired so on Michael. It was plain orange, almost like a carrot. She had to admit he was almost as handsome as Michael; and when he found her gaze and smiled, she felt her heart warm to the kindness reflected in his clear green eyes.

He shifted his eyes and scanned the room. "Shall we stand and say the Lord's Prayer?"

Amid the shuffle of the congregation rising to its feet, Aimee leaned closer with a grin. "See? I told you."

Miss Hannah scowled at the top of Aimee's head, and Star felt compelled to place a finger to her lips to shush the girl.

As one voice, the members of the small church offered the prayer. Though she only comprehended part of their meaning, her pulse quickened at the reverence displayed in the hushed tones.

In this place, she felt clean, as though perhaps it didn't matter quite so much that her mother had sold herself to men, and maybe it was okay that Star didn't know who her father was. And maybe, just maybe, she had finally found a place to belong.

As in a beautiful dream, Star floated through the service on a beam of wonder. The singing lifted her beyond anything she had ever experienced, causing her to positively ache with joy.

Though she had spent her life listening to lively, bawdy tunes in the saloons, she had never known the beauty of voices lifted in praise. She felt God must be sitting back in heaven and smiling at the wondrous sound.

And the preaching! How could one man take the Good Book and cause it to come so alive in a few short moments? Yet, that was exactly what Reverend Hank had done.

Over and over, Star allowed her gaze to drift to her open Bible so she might reread the text: *"Trust in the Lord with all thine heart; and lean not unto thine own understanding. In all thy ways acknowledge him, and he shall direct thy paths."*

In the weeks she had been reading the Bible, Star had never read anything so utterly comforting—that God was able to direct her path. And that's what He had done so far.

Though her heart still ached at the loss of her mother, and tears still flowed during moments of solitude, Star was learning to accept her circumstances and looked forward to her new lessons each day. She'd been learning the Scriptures and started to do some of the chores; and through it all, God had truly opened up a whole new life for her. She embraced each new day.

When the service was over, Star stood outside on the church steps with Michael, Miss Hannah, and Aimee. Star's mouth curved into a timid smile as the little girl proudly introduced Star to the preacher.

Hank smiled warmly. "I apologize for not getting out to the farm to meet you sooner, Miss Campbell."

"I—it's okay," she said, ducking her head and feeling perfectly unworthy to be standing before such a good man. "A man such as yourself has more important things to attend to."

"Well, I'd like to make it up to you." He glanced past her. "Ma, how about if we all go over and eat dinner at Joe's? My treat."

"Pay for a meal when we have perfectly good food at

home?" Miss Hannah sounded scandalized. "You come on out to the farm, and I'll make you a nice home-cooked meal."

"Now, Ma," he said with a teasing grin. "You wouldn't deny your son the pleasure of showing off his lovely mother to the folks, would you?"

A blush stained Ma's weathered cheeks. "Oh, go on, sweet talker. Just like your pa." Her fond gaze belied her scolding tone. With a grumpy sigh, she shook her head and waved a plump hand. "All right then, but I have it from a very reliable source that the prices that man charges are plumb outrageous."

"Mrs. Merlin, eh?" Hank chuckled. "It looks to me like she's headed over there, so the two of you will have a lot to talk about next time you make a trip to the mercantile."

Michael chuckled too.

"Shall we head over to the restaurant?" Hank asked.

"I still say it's nonsense to pay someone else to cook a meal when a body has two perfectly good hands, but if you insist. . ."

Michael and Hank grinned at each other over Miss Hannah's gray head.

The men each took up a place on either side of their mother, and Star grasped Aimee's hand, trailing after them.

Once they had crossed the dusty street, Aimee ran on ahead while Star hung back, enjoying the coolness of the autumn air as she surveyed the town. She passed the mercantile and the bank, then continued forward.

To Star's surprise, the door hung open at the next shop she came to. The sign above the door read *Rosemary's Creations*, and Star could only surmise that this was the seamstress whom Aimee thought lovely and the rest of the town believed had no business being single.

From within, voices carried to the wooden sidewalk.

"Well, I still don't think it's very proper for a young lady to be living out there with a widowed man and his daughter."

Star stopped in her tracks. Curiously, she pressed herself against the building and peeked inside.

"I mean, what is Michael thinking?" The woman who spoke could have been eighteen or thirty. Star couldn't tell past the sour expression marring a face that might have been attractive, had she smiled. "A person would expect the preacher's brother to think a little more about keeping up appearances."

"I'm sure Mr. Riley knows what he is doing, and his mother is there too," a quiet voice spoke. "And the young lady seems to be a fine girl. I wouldn't worry about the preacher's reputation if I were you, though it's awfully kind of you to be so concerned."

Star viewed her champion. Her blond hair was swept up into a chignon and netted at the nape of her neck. Star had trouble believing behind the gentle face lurked a "teeerrrible" secret as Aimee had disclosed earlier.

An unladylike snort left the other woman's lips. "But did you see how she sat next to Aimee and held her hand through the service?" She sniffed. "As though she was the child's mother. If you ask me, that girl is fishing for a husband and thinks Michael would be a good catch."

Star bit her lip to hold back a gasp. What nerve! She was hard-pressed to keep from stomping in there and telling that woman just what she thought of her opinions, and probably would have done just that if not for the soft voice drifting through the doorway.

"Anyone would be blind not to see that Mr. Riley is a good catch, but that doesn't mean every available woman is looking to catch him." The pleasant woman's voice had taken on a tone that Star could only describe as irritated. "Maybe we should wait until we get to know the new girl before we judge her too harshly."

"Well, there's no need to get snippy."

"I apologize, Mrs. Slavens. But Mrs. Barker will have dinner on the table, and she gets mighty upset if her boarders are late. So if the gown is to your satisfaction. . ."

"Oh, dear me, yes. It's lovely. I do appreciate your opening the shop for me on the Lord's Day. I could never have made a trip to Portland without that dress."

"It was my pleasure, I assure you. And I truly hope your mother's broken leg heals quickly so you may return to our fair town without delay."

"Why, thank you, Dear," Mrs. Slavens returned, a flush of pleasure sweeping her pinched cheeks. "How sweet of you to say so."

"Coming, Star?"

Star jumped as Michael's voice called to her. Glancing toward the sound of his voice, Star caught his questioning frown from down the block. A blush burned her cheeks as she darted a gaze back inside the shop, praying they hadn't heard.

But they had.

Both women stood mutely observing her. Catching the haughty expression on Mrs. Slavens's face, Star jutted her chin and moved to join the Rileys, wishing for all she was worth that she hadn't stopped to eavesdrop in the first place.

eight

Tears slipped down Star's face as she forced her feet to carry her the two miles to Hobbs. Overhearing the conversation at the dressmaker's yesterday had confirmed what she'd known all along and refused to admit to herself. She couldn't continue to take refuge and charity from Michael and Miss Hannah one more day. Not when she ran the risk of besmirching Michael's good name by her mere presence in the house.

Lying awake, watching moonbeams dance across her bedroom ceiling, she'd made the decision to leave the security and warmth of Michael's home.

An hour later, after dressing in the drab gray dress and packing the even uglier brown, she waited until she heard Michael rise, start a fire in the kitchen stove, and head out to do chores. When the door closed behind him, she crept through the house and stepped into the cold morning air. Now, as she neared town, streaks of pink were just beginning to stretch across the gray sky, but even the beauty of awakening dawn did nothing to improve her dismal outlook.

She breathed only a small sigh of relief when the town loomed before her. She certainly didn't look forward to serving food to people like that hateful Slavens woman. But what other choice did she have? Even with her newly acquired sewing skills, she wasn't experienced enough to do it for a living. Except for serving food and drinks, she had no other skills to speak of. The saloon was out of the question, but the service at the restaurant the day before had been so poor, Star figured she could get a job easily and probably do a lot to improve the quality of the cafe.

Few people occupied the streets this early, but shops were beginning to open. A smile tipped Star's lips. Aimee had mourned for two days upon finding out she would have to wait another year to go to school.

Memories replayed in Star's mind. Memories of laughter, love, stories, and evening Bible reading. Michael and Miss Hannah answered question after question for Star. Her heart swelled with hope for her future; and although she felt a physical pain at the move away from the Rileys' farm, peace permeated her spirit.

"Trust in the Lord with all thine heart ;and lean not unto thine own understanding. In all thy ways acknowledge Him, and He shall direct thy paths."

A deep, cleansing breath lifted, then lowered Star's chest. She trusted Him. Hadn't He guided her to Michael and Miss Hannah in the first place? Hadn't He allowed her time to learn His Holy Word? Of course she had a lot more to learn, but she almost never swore anymore. When she did, she immediately repented—even if there was no one around to hear the offending words. She was beginning to recognize that prick of conscience when she committed infractions. Like three mornings ago. Cannonball had jumped on her when she was walking from the henhouse with the morning eggs. She'd been so mad that he'd dirtied her freshly washed dress, she pitched three of the eggs, hitting the bewildered animal before she realized what she was doing and hurried into the house.

When Miss Hannah remarked over the fewer than usual number of eggs, Star had blurted out that this surprised her as well and perhaps the hens required more feed. Knowing that by not telling the whole truth, she was lying, Star went about the rest of her morning chores in miserable silence. At breakfast, when Michael asked her to say the morning blessing, Star burst into tears and confessed about the three wasted eggs and how she'd let her temper get the better of her. As penance, she offered her breakfast to Michael to make up for the extra two eggs glaringly absent on his plate.

Michael's lips twitched as he told her he thought four would be plenty this morning, but to try to control her temper and not throw their breakfast at Cannonball from now on.

Oh, how she had tried to slow her quickening pulse when he'd winked at her to let her know he was teasing. Even now, just picturing his gentle brown eyes, her heart picked up a beat.

Immersed in the sweet memories, Star almost passed the restaurant. Had she not smelled bread baking within, she might have missed it altogether. She stopped short at the door. Reaching forward, she tried to gain entrance, but the knob refused to turn. She knocked hard and waited, then knocked again.

"Who's down there?" an abrupt female voice called from somewhere above Star. "We don't open for dinner until eleven."

Star stepped back and tipped her head so she could see to the second floor of the building. "Wait!" she called as the shutters started to close. They opened again, and Star recognized Jane, the young woman who had served their inadequate meal the day before.

"What do you want?" she asked with a scowl.

Star's heart beat a rapid cadence within her chest. Oh, why did Jane have to be the nasty sort? Groveling for a job was going to be difficult enough as it was.

"Well?"

"I–I'm looking for a position. I thought there might be something available for me here."

"Why would you think that?" The hostility radiating from the girl could heat the coldest room.

Star's cheeks warmed. She knew she couldn't very well insult Jane's serving skills, so she just shrugged. "I don't know. I ate here yesterday and noticed how busy you were." She gave her best effort at a friendly smile. "Your customers surely were running you ragged. I–I thought maybe you could use some help."

Jane gave a sniff. "If you didn't like the service, you could have eaten at home."

"No! Th—that's not what I—" But it was too late. The shutter slammed, cutting her off midexplanation.

Stomping her foot in frustration, Star spun around and took a second to swipe the town with her gaze. Across the street, a man stumbled from the saloon. He boldly raked her with a hot look and tipped his hat in drunken approval, despite Star's plain attire and pinched hairdo. Thankfully, he didn't attempt conversation. Star shuddered, her mind replaying every night of serving drinks in Luke's Saloon over the past two years. She'd never go back to that! But what if she couldn't find a position somewhere? Panic exploded in her chest, sending tremors of fear and dread through her belly. Would she be forced to serve drinks again?

She dipped her head and prayed a quick, silent prayer for help.

"Why, hello."

Star jerked her head up in surprise. The seamstress stood only a few feet from her on the boardwalk, getting ready to enter her shop. Her lovely smile warmed Star immediately.

"Hello," she replied.

"Joe doesn't open for breakfast. As a matter of fact, he refuses to come to the door one second before eleven."

"Oh, I wasn't waiting for breakfast. I, well, as a matter of fact, I was hoping Joe might hire me. But his daughter—" Star's voice trailed as she gave a helpless little wave toward the upstairs window.

"Yes, I saw. . ." A look of sympathy crossed Rosemary's features, and she nodded. "My name's Rosemary."

"Star," she mumbled and waited for the raised eyebrow her unusual name typically brought.

Rosemary only gave her a pleasant smile. "What a lovely name. How about joining me for a cup of tea, Star? Jane obviously isn't going to inform her pa you're waiting to speak to him, so you'll have to wait until he opens for business."

"I—I don't know, I really should try to knock again."

With hands on her slender hips, Rosemary gave her a firm look. "Joe will be clanging away in the kitchen, preparing whatever he plans to serve later. You could knock until your knuckles bleed and never get an answer. Besides, you must give me the opportunity to make up for my unspeakable rudeness yesterday."

Heat sprouted to Star's face. "There's no need—"

Closing the distance between them, Rosemary slipped her arm around Star's shoulders. "Pshaw, of course there's need. I'd planned a little trip out to the Riley farm later to apologize anyway. This is ever so much better, because now I can treat you to a nice cup of tea, and we can get to know each other without an audience."

Overcome by the unaccustomed kindness from a respectable and beautiful woman, Star almost broke down and wept. Instead, she reined in her emotions, smiled and nodded. "All right. I'd appreciate it."

"Wonderful!" Rosemary beamed as though she truly was delighted. Star felt she had no reason to doubt the dressmaker's sincerity.

Inside the snug little shop, Rosemary removed her gloves and rubbed her hands together. "Mornings are getting a bit chillier as the days grow shorter. I'll have a fire on in no time. Would you be a dear and get some water for the teakettle? The pump is out back."

By the time Star returned, a small fire burned in the woodstove. Rosemary beamed, her smile lifting Star's spirits and assuring her everything would be all right.

Taking the teakettle, Rosemary motioned toward a small straight-backed wooden chair. "Go ahead and sit down," she said. "The water will take a few moments to boil."

"Thank you." Star sat gratefully. The two-mile walk into town had tired her out more than she'd realized, and a hot spot on her big toe felt suspiciously as though it might become a blister inside the slightly large boots Michael had purchased for her.

Rosemary brought a stool from the other side of the room and set it down close to Star. "Now, tell me why you're looking for work. Did the Rileys turn you out?"

"Oh, no! Of course not!"

"I didn't think so, but I wanted to be sure."

Heat crept up Star's neck and warmed her cheeks once more. Rosemary obviously meant she wanted to be sure Michael hadn't turned her out for a good reason. As embarrassing as it was, Star couldn't blame her. "No, I just felt I could no longer accept their kindness."

"But weren't you staying there to help Miss Hannah? I was under the impression they hired you as sort of a housemaid."

A rueful smile tipped Star's lips. "Miss Hannah gets along just fine. She works circles around me. I suspect they only invented a position so that I wouldn't feel like I was accepting charity." As soon as she spoke the words, Star worried she might sound ungrateful and hurried to clarify. "Miss Hannah and Michael are the kindest, most generous people I've ever known, besides my own mother. I simply couldn't accept their generosity any longer." She glanced at Rosemary, silently beseeching the dressmaker to try to understand and not ask too many questions.

"I see. And does this sudden decision have anything to do with the conversation you overheard yesterday?"

Star averted her gaze to her hands. "I suppose," she mumbled.

"Honey, there will always be gossips who delight in speculating. Moving into town won't stop tongues from wagging about you."

Jerking her head up to meet Rosemary's gaze, Star regarded her earnestly. "Yes, but this way, they are only talking about me, and they can leave Michael out of it."

"Oh. I see."

And Star could tell by the raised brow and knowing lift of her chin that Rosemary indeed saw much more than Star would ever have revealed had she not been so annoyingly transparent.

"And does Michael feel the same way about you?" Her eyes twinkled and a teasing smile curved her lips.

"Oh, no!" Star couldn't bear the thought of Michael's good name being dragged through the mud on her account. Better to spell it out right up front. Maybe Rosemary could pass along the information. "Michael is much too fine a man to fall in love with the likes of me. I—I heard him tell Miss Hannah he was going to begin looking for a proper wife for him and mother for little Aimee."

How her stomach clenched at the very thought of another woman filling that role. Despite knowing she had no business even allowing herself to think about it, Star had been unable to stop the dream of occupying that place in their lives. She heaved a sigh and glanced up to find Rosemary's sympathetic gaze studying her. Star cleared her throat. "So, you see, Michael has no idea how I feel about him. I have no intention of ever making a fool of myself and admitting it. I only hope it's not so obvious to everyone else."

Rosemary's pleasant laughter filled the air. "I have a knack for picking up on this sort of thing. Don't worry. Your secret is perfectly safe with me."

Star couldn't resist returning her grin. "That's a relief."

Steam lifted from the kettle bringing an end to the embarrassing conversation. Rosemary stood. "I love tea. There's just something about a cup that cheers me right up on a gloomy day."

A couple of moments later, she returned with two dainty cups, each sitting primly on a matching saucer.

Star took hers and studied the hand-painted roses. "This is lovely."

"Thank you." Sadness darkened Rosemary's sunny expression. "They were my mother's. I inherited the entire set of china when she passed on."

"Oh, I'm so sorry. I lost my own mother recently. Sometimes I miss her so much, I think my heart will break in two."

"We will have to be there to support one another." Rosemary's gentle voice felt like a comforting embrace.

Swallowing back the sudden lump in her throat, Star nodded and sipped at her tea.

Obviously sensing her need for another topic, Rosemary gave a bright smile. "Well, now, have you found a place to stay?"

Star blinked at her. "Wh–why no. I hadn't thought that far ahead. I assumed if I got the job, I'd have a place to stay above the restaurant."

Rosemary gave a careless wave. "Honey, even if Joe had room upstairs, believe me, you don't want to live there."

Imagining Jane's scowling face, Star shuddered. Rosemary was more than likely right about that. "Then what do you suggest?"

A warm smile curved Rosemary's lips. "It just so happens that I have too much space in my room at the boarding-house. I could easily move a cot in there for you. How about moving in with me and sharing expenses?"

Star's stomach sank, and she dropped her gaze to the cup and saucer in her lap. Her mind went to the few small coins in her bag. "I am afraid I don't. . ." Her cheeks warmed.

"Oh, don't worry about that for now."

Stiffening her back, Star regarded Rosemary with a frank stare. "I couldn't take charity, though I do appreciate the kindness."

"Don't be silly. You can't sleep on the street, can you?"

"I don't suppose."

"Tell you what: This place is such a pigsty, I can hardly find my shears. What if you clean it up for me? That would be worth at least your share of rent for a week."

Star cast a dubious glance about the spotless shop. Pigsty indeed. She regarded Rosemary frankly. "Why are you doing this?"

"Let's just say, if I'd had a friend when I first came to Hobbs a few months ago, things might have gone much smoother for me." Her lips tilted into a grin, and her eyes widened in mock horror. "Imagine a woman living alone and choosing to be an old maid! I declare, I simply *must* be hiding something!"

A giggle burst from Star at Rosemary's version of little Aimee's tale surrounding the dressmaker.

"I see you've already heard the rumors." The statement held no animosity, only a lacing of humor behind the husky tone.

"I'm sorry. If it means anything to you, I didn't put much stock in what I heard. I don't really think you're hiding anything."

The dressmaker's eyes twinkled in response. "One of the most important things my mother ever told me was, 'Sweetie, folks will always love to tell tales about anyone different. The most important thing to remember is never, ever give them a real reason to talk.'"

"Then it doesn't bother you what they say?"

A wistful sigh escaped Rosemary's lips. "I suppose it does sometimes. I don't have a lot of friends among the women of this town." She lifted her brow. "They keep me in business, so I shouldn't complain. So, what do you say? Help me for a few hours, and you can stay with me at the boardinghouse."

Reluctantly, Star accepted the kind offer.

She spent the rest of the morning sweeping up nonexistent dirt from the floor, wiping nonexistent dust from the shelves, and refolding perfectly neat piles of dress goods.

At eleven, she walked into Joe's Restaurant, determined not to take no for an answer.

ፚ

Michael muttered to himself as he pulled up to the restaurant and tethered the team of horses to the hitching post. Only the memory of Aimee's tears and Ma's insistence that he "not come home without her" kept him from turning around and leaving Star to her own devices. If the girl was so ungrateful that she could walk away without so much as an explanation, then as far as he was concerned, she could just work in a sweltering kitchen and serve beef stew to the townsfolk.

What did it matter to him? Surely he'd done more than God expected of him. He'd taken her in, bought her clothing. But the memory of her bright face when she'd tried on the green muslin gown reminded him exactly why he cared enough to put aside his plowing for the rest of the day and follow her into town like a loyal dog. Star's laughter lifted his spirits at least once every single day. Her beauty never failed to trigger a rise in his pulse—no matter how carefully she tried to conceal it. He didn't have the heart to tell her that, despite her efforts, she was still lovelier than the prettiest flower ever to grow.

For weeks, she had woven her life with his so tightly, he'd come to expect her presence as a matter of course. Like Ma and Aimee. He resented her absence deeply enough that he'd paced at breakfast, unable to eat, and then again at lunch, until Ma had insisted he come to town, find Star, and bring her home.

He hadn't had to be told twice. All the way to town, he'd practiced telling her how much they had come to care for her as part of the family and how Ma needed her there. But as he stepped toward the door to Joe's, his forlornness had changed to anger. He had no intention of begging her to come home. He was going to tell it to her like it was, and she'd better not argue.

What had she expected? That he would just let her go? That in a town the size of Hobbs, he couldn't find out from one stop at the mercantile where she was? Mrs. Merlin had delighted in telling him exactly what Star had been up to. Working! As a serving girl at Joe's!

"Good afternoon, Mr. Riley."

Snatching his hand back from the door, he turned to find Miss Rosemary smiling at him from her shop next door. He lifted his hat from his head. "Good afternoon."

"Are you heading into Joe's for a late lunch or an early supper?" Her eyes twinkled merrily, and Michael could have sworn amusement hung on her words.

"No, I'm looking for someone."

"Anyone in particular?"

"Well, yes. Of course." Michael frowned. Why did women have to be so nosy anyway? "I'm looking for the young woman who accompanied my family to church yesterday. I heard she's found herself a job at Joe's. I have to go and talk to her."

"Why not wait until her workday is over? You know how Joe is, Mr. Riley. If you interfere with Star's work, he might find it an excuse to fire her. And then where would she be?"

"It doesn't matter. I'm here to take her home anyway."

"Oh? And what if she prefers to live and work in town?"

Michael let out a snort before he could stop himself. "I beg your pardon for my lack of manners, Miss, but why would anyone rather serve food for a man like Joe than be a part of a family?"

Rosemary tilted her head and regarded him evenly. "She isn't a part of your family, Mr. Riley. She knows that, and the folks in town know it. She's saving you from gossip. I must say, I admire her a great deal for it."

Gaping, Michael watched her speak and forced himself to assimilate her words. "So you're saying she left for my sake?"

"That, and because she just knew it was the right thing to do."

"It wasn't the right thing," Michael protested. "We need her."

"She doesn't feel that you do."

Michael scowled. "How do you know all of this, anyway?"

"Let's just say Star and I got to know each other pretty well this morning before Joe hired her."

"Well, I've known her for a lot longer than a few hours, and I say she'd be better off where I can keep an eye on her."

"I see. And are you prepared to offer her a proposal, Mr. Riley?"

"A proposal for what?"

She smiled pointedly.

Michael's neck warmed as her inference hit him smack in the gut. "Of course not!"

"Oh? Because she isn't the 'proper sort of wife for you and the proper sort of mother for Aimee?'" Her words rang with challenge. "It seems to me, for a man not willing to officially make her part of the family, you're awfully possessive."

Indignation burned within his breast. "That's my business, Miss. Not yours. Now if you'll excuse me, I'll collect Star and be on my way."

"Very well, Mr. Riley. Do what you feel you must. But please consider something first: Star has made arrangements to share my room at the boardinghouse, she is gainfully employed, and I'm guessing for the first time in her life she is feeling a sense of accomplishment. Perhaps if you would put her needs above your own, you would see that this just might be the best thing she could have done."

Resentment boiled inside Michael, and he fought to be civil. What would he expect from a woman who clearly chose to live and work alone? He'd never been one to put much stock in idle gossip, but perhaps in this case. . .

He jerked a nod toward her. "Thank you for your advice, Miss," Michael said tersely. "Good day."

But her words strung a trail of reason through his brain. Did Star actually *prefer* working at Joe's and living at the boardinghouse? He almost convinced himself to return to the farm and come back later after Star was able to leave for the day when he saw her. She came through the kitchen door, carrying a tray. His heart clenched at the sight of her. Sweat beaded her brow and strands of hair had come loose from her tight bun and framed her face in ringlets. Weariness showed plainly in her eyes and the slump of her shoulders. Michael could see she tried desperately to keep up with the yelling Joe in the back and the equally demanding customers in the dining room. "Hurry up, Girl!" a man called across the room. "I ain't got all day!"

Rosemary's words of reasoning fled Michael's mind at the abuse Star was taking. He'd had all he could abide. In a few short strides, he reached Star and grabbed hold of her arm. "Come on, we're going home!"

She gasped and turned sharply. "Michael!"

Heat seared Michael's chest as a steaming bowl of beef stew slid down his shirt.

nine

Star stared in horror at Michael.

He winced at what must surely burn like fire.

"What are you doing here?" she whispered, though she doubted he could hear her through the raucous laughter filling the dining room—completely at Michael's expense.

"I came to take you home," he replied through gritted teeth.

Resenting his assumption that she would jump at the chance to return to the farm, Star nevertheless couldn't help the thrill she felt that he'd come after her.

He pulled out his handkerchief and uselessly rubbed at the mess down the front of his shirt. "Doesn't look like you're cut out for this kind of job anyway."

"I wouldn't have spilled the food if you hadn't pulled my arm and scared me half to death."

He glowered. "Is that so?"

"Yes," she snapped back. "I am good at serving customers. It's what I did at Luke's. . . ." She broke off and clamped her lips together. Clearing her throat, she then slowly forced herself to meet his inquisitive gaze.

"You didn't leave so much as a note."

The quiet statement sent a quiver through her stomach. "I know, and that was wrong of me. I should have explained."

Stepping closer, he towered above her, taking Star's breath away. "Explain now."

"Hey, Girl! Is that my food your beau's wearing?"

The room erupted in renewed laughter.

Dread wormed its way through her stomach as Joe appeared at the kitchen door, obviously summoned by the noise.

"What's going on out here?" he demanded, then seeing

Michael's shirt, he scowled. "Guess I just lost me another worthless serving girl."

"No, please!"

"It was my fault, Joe. I grabbed her arm."

The grizzled cook glanced from one to the other, grunted, and fixed his gaze on Star. "That's coming out of yer pay. Get back here and dish up another bowl. Harvey ain't gonna wait all day."

"Yes, Sir," Star replied, her cheeks burning under the reprimand.

"Jane!" Joe bellowed. "Get out here and clean up that mess the new girl just made."

"Please, don't bother Jane. I'll clean it up in a jiffy—just as soon as I take Harvey a fresh bowl of stew."

"You got yer hands full. Or are you trying to tell me how to run my business? I fired the last girl because she thought she knew how to run the business better than me."

"Oh, no, Sir!"

"Fine." He closed the kitchen door, but his voice slammed through the wood and filled the entire dining room as he hollered once more. "Jane! Get down here and clean up this mess!"

Never in all her years of serving food at Luke's had Star spilled anything on a customer. Now Michael had to go and make her look incompetent. She turned her glare upon him. Gathering a deep breath for control, she focused on keeping her voice calm. "I am sorry I didn't say good-bye. It was truly inexcusable. But as you can see, I have my hands full at the moment."

He scowled. "Would it interest you to know that Aimee cried because you left?"

"She did?" Oh, the darling child. Star already missed her terribly.

"Yes, she did. And Ma wants you to come back. She told me not to come home without you."

Star's heart sank. "Excuse me, Michael. I have to go and dish up another bowl of stew." Giving him no chance to protest, Star retrieved the dishes from the floor and headed into the back room.

Disappointment sang a bitter song inside of her head. So he hadn't come to bring her back because he cared for her and missed her himself. He was simply doing his mother's bidding. At least Miss Hannah and Aimee loved her. Would it have made a difference if he'd come of his own volition? Perhaps. But Star knew God had led her to leave, had led her to Rosemary, and even Joe's, though she hated the job already and she had only been working for three hours.

When she returned to the dining room, Michael stood in exactly the same place she'd left him. "I need to speak with you," he growled.

A heavy sigh escaped Star's lips. "Michael, I can't talk now. You'll either have to wait or leave."

"Fine," he said with a stubborn tightening of his jaw. "I'll wait." He located an empty table and sat in a chair next to it.

Without another glance in Michael's direction, Star delivered the food to her disgruntled customer and caught up with the rest of her work. A good twenty minutes later, Michael still sat alone at the table, scowling.

She gathered a steadying breath and walked toward him.

"Now, let me explain," she said. "I appreciate your kindness more than you'll ever know, Michael. I know how blessed I am that God saw fit to lead you to me and that you saw fit to put me in your wagon and save me from Clem and Luke."

"Then how could you leave?" He glanced purposefully around the dining room. "I know we don't have a fancy home, but surely it's preferable to this sort of life."

"I suppose that depends on your perspective." Star's defenses rose a bit at his superior tone. "There's nothing wrong with a person putting in a hard day's work—even if that work includes serving food and cleaning up after people." She gave a short laugh. "That's what wives do all day. It's good, honest work."

"Is that what you think being a wife is? Just a lot of work equal to this sort of life?"

"That's not what I—"

But he gave her no chance to finish. He stood, towering above her. "I'll tell Ma you've made your choice. I hope you don't live to regret it." With that, he turned and strode through the room and left without looking back.

Tears pricked Star's eyes, but there was no time to allow them free rein as a half dozen more customers walked through the door and demanded her attention. Grateful for the diversion, Star immersed herself in keeping Joe and the diners satisfied. It was after eight when the last customer left. Star spent the next two hours cleaning the dining room, washing dishes, and restocking supplies for the following day. When she stepped outside, it was past eleven. She was weary to her bones, but satisfied that she'd put in a good day's labor.

Though the night was chilly, she couldn't help but enjoy the fresh air. She gathered a few deep, cleansing breaths.

"Star?"

She jumped. "Oh, Michael. You nearly scared the life out of me."

"Lucky for me you didn't have hot food in your hands."

"What are you doing in town? You must be dog tired."

"I came back in after supper. I brought the rest of your things."

"I brought everything that belongs to me."

"What about the Bible I gave you or the two pretty dresses you and Ma made?"

Star glanced at the ground. "I didn't want you to feel as though I took advantage."

"Who else is going to wear them?"

He had a point there. Star smiled and nodded. "All right. I'll pay you back as I'm paid."

Michael scowled. "We'll discuss that at a later time. As far as the Bible goes, that was a gift. I want you to have it."

Unable to refuse, Star nodded again. "Thank you, Michael. I'll take good care of it, and if you ever need it or want it back, I promise not to make a fuss."

With an exasperated sigh, Michael reached out and captured her chin between his thumb and forefinger, forcing her to meet his gaze. "I will never take that Bible away from you. Get that through your head. It's yours forever—or for however long you'd like to keep it."

"I'll keep it forever," she whispered, her heart beating so fast she thought she might pass out from the sheer joy of his soft touch. The way his eyes studied her face, the sudden intake of his breath as his gaze lowered to her mouth, made her legs go weak.

He released her chin and motioned toward the road. "Come on to the wagon, and I'll drive you over to the boardinghouse."

Fighting disappointment, Star slipped her hand inside the arm he gallantly offered. "How did you know I'm staying there?"

"Rosemary caught me earlier and explained that you were going to share her room."

He helped her to the wagon seat.

As she watched him walk around to his side and climb up, Star was struck by a painfully brilliant idea. She was never going to be the sort of woman Michael had in mind for a wife. Even if by some miracle he fell in love with her, once he found out about Mama and Luke and the real reason Clem had been following her, he would be horrified and never speak to her again. Rosemary was everything a man like Michael could want in a wife, and Aimee would adore her. After all, hadn't she already said Miss Rosemary was beautiful?

"Michael?"

"Yeah?" The wagon lurched forward as he flapped the reins.

Even in the pale light of the moon, his handsome face caused her heart to still and she almost changed her mind. But she bravely forged ahead at the thought of little Aimee and her need for a good ma.

"What do you think of Rosemary?"

"I hardly ever think about her at all. Why do you ask?"

"I don't know. Just wondering."

"I suppose she's a mite opinionated."

"But you like that. At least we've had some lively discussions."

"Well. . .I reckon that's true. What brought this on, anyway?"

"I heard from Rosemary today that the lady's society is hosting a bazaar to raise money to build the new school next summer. That way, the church won't have to serve as the school too."

"Yeah, Hank and I discussed it this evening while I was waiting for you."

"I'm sure Rosemary doesn't have an escort."

"You think Hank should ask her? As a matter of fact, that's not a bad idea. Ma's been pestering him something awful about a preacher needing a wife." He grinned. "Look at us, playing matchmakers."

Letting out a frustrated breath, she decided to take a more direct approach. "But, Michael, don't you think Rosemary's pretty?"

He shrugged. "I suppose she's pleasing to the eye. Come to think of it, I guess she's more than a little pretty, isn't she? I never thought of it before."

Star wasn't prepared for the pain his honest words would inflict, and she couldn't bring herself to go through with it. She'd planted a seed. Her part was done. Should he take the hint and invite Rosemary to the bazaar, Star would try her best not to let jealousy come between her and her new friend. Somehow she couldn't help but hope Rosemary would take a liking to the parson and leave Michael alone.

❧

Michael gathered a deep breath as he watched Star walk into the boardinghouse. Mrs. Barker, the dragon who ran the place, stood at the door in her nightcap, clutching her dressing gown to her throat as though he might ravage her any second. Comical as that might be, Michael resented anyone refusing him access to Star. For the past weeks, he'd had the benefit of her company whenever he wished. And often when he didn't particularly wish, but at least there hadn't been this constant ache he now felt in her absence.

Just why he should feel this way about a girl like Star, he wasn't sure. He'd be a fool and a liar to try to make anyone believe he wasn't drawn to her beauty. She was an uncommon beauty, despite her obvious attempts to make herself plain. Why she was trying to make herself look like Mrs. Barker was beyond him. But there was more to it than merely a physical attraction. He looked forward to hearing about Aimee's antics from Star's animated lips. Ma did a fair amount of talking about his daughter's adventures, but not with the delight with which Star could weave a tale. Star spoke with all the love, pride, and indulgence of a doting mother.

A frown creased Michael's brow, and he urged the horses faster. A doting mother? Where had such an ignorant thought come from? Star. . .a mother. Beautiful, childlike Star who knew nothing about being a mother. Half the time, she seemed more like an older sister to Aimee. How old was she anyway? Eighteen? Well, that was old enough, he supposed. He'd been barely more than that when he married Sarah. But what about her manners, her swearing? He had to admit, though, it had been a long time since he'd heard a curse word fly past those beautiful, rosebud lips.

A war raged inside of him the rest of the way home. On one hand, Star was a breath of fresh spring air. She filled his senses every waking moment and his dreams at night. She loved his daughter and the feeling was mutual. His mother felt Star could do no wrong and had come to the conclusion that if she'd stolen anything, it was with a right good reason, and Ma chose to forget it.

Problem was, Michael couldn't forget. If he didn't have an impressionable daughter to consider, things might be different; but for all of her softening and apparent spiritual growth, Star still hadn't opened up about anything in her past. She hadn't confessed about stealing. The times he'd hinted at it, she'd quickly changed the subject.

Michael's heavy heart grew even heavier and by the time he got the horses bedded down for the night and entered the house, he was convinced more than ever that Star couldn't be the woman for him. Though he strongly felt God had brought Star into their lives, he had to be realistic. No matter how his sentimental heart wished otherwise, she wasn't his. They had rescued her and introduced her to the Word and helped her understand fundamental truths about being a Christian. Now God had sent her out on her own like a baby bird leaving the nest. Would she fly or come crashing down and return to her life of thievery?

"Well? Where is she?"

Ma's demanding voice startled him. "What are you doing up?"

"Do you think I could sleep without knowing when Star's coming home?"

"As I told you earlier, she made her decision."

Ma heaved a sigh and plopped down in a chair by the table. "I had hoped she would change her mind and come on home with you. It's amazing how easily the heart attaches itself to another heart, isn't it?"

"I suppose." Michael knew better than to agree too readily, though Ma pretty much summed it up. His heart was attached to Star. It would be awhile before he was able to detach. It wouldn't do anyone a bit of good to let Ma in on that fact.

"Well, what are you going to do about it?"

"What do you mean? There's nothing else I can do. Last I heard, kidnapping is a crime."

"Aren't you just the clever one?" Ma's wounded tone shamed Michael.

"I'm sorry. I didn't mean to sass. But, truly, Ma, there's nothing we can do to keep her here if she wants to leave. She feels she needs to make it on her own."

"Hogwash. She feels uncomfortable living with a widower, his daughter, and mother. She doesn't believe we really need her, and all the funny looks she received yesterday at service made her feel like an outsider."

"What looks?" Michael scowled, indignation rising in his breast. Who had the nerve to give Star any *looks?*

Ma rolled her eyes. "You men don't notice anything unless it smacks you on the head."

"Rosemary said Star left for our sakes."

Ma nodded. "I figured as much. She doesn't want folks suggesting improper things about you."

Michael's neck warmed. "Who would think anything improper is going on with my ma and little girl in the house?"

"Just about everyone, I'd venture to guess. That's just the nature of things. I'm ashamed to say, I might think the same thing in their position. Star is a beautiful young woman, and you are a handsome and lonely widower."

"Ma!"

"Oh, now. You're a grown man. Don't play innocent with me. I know you're a decent man and would never take advantage of a situation like this. Anyone should know that after you married that floozy instead of just—"

"Ma. . ."

"I'm sorry. You're right. I shouldn't speak ill of the dead."

"You shouldn't speak ill of anyone, but that's not the point. Sarah was Aimee's mother, and I don't ever want Aimee to feel she has cause to be ashamed. I don't want to chance her overhearing the truth about her ma."

Ma reached over and covered Michael's hand. "You're a good man, Son. I know God has a woman for you. You deserve some happiness."

Michael retreated inwardly, waiting. . . .

"I'd hoped that maybe you'd cast your attention toward Star."

Clearing his throat, Michael turned his hand over and squeezed Ma's. "She isn't right for Aimee and me."

"Why? Because she's beautiful? Or because she wasn't nursed on the Ten Commandments?"

"Because the only thing I know about her is that she's accused of being a thief, and I'm not convinced the man was lying."

"Then why don't you just ask her about it? If she admits to it, why then you have proof that she's changed. If she denies it, then the man was lying."

"What if she's the one lying?"

Standing, Ma gave a careless wave. "Star couldn't tell a lie to save her life." She shook her head and chuckled. "Remember the other day when she pelted Cannonball with eggs?"

Unable to resist the sweet memory, Michael laughed outright. "Poor Cannonball was forced to have a bath. I don't think he'll ever forgive her."

"My point is that her conscience won't allow her to do anything that she feels is a sin."

Cynicism returning in full force, Michael snorted. "Maybe she doesn't feel stealing is a sin. Have you checked your valuables?"

Eyes narrowing, Ma shook her finger. "I am ashamed of you. You know that sweet girl would rather chop off her hand than to do anything to hurt this family—or anyone else, I'd vow. You can deny that you care about her all you want, but I'll not have you implying anything improper about her character in my presence. You're so concerned with what Aimee might think of her mother, well, let me tell you, Star has been more of a ma to that child than Sarah ever could have been. It would hurt Aimee much more to hear her pa saying hateful things against Star than the ma she never knew."

Giving him no chance to apologize, Ma spun around with a surprising agility, given her girth, and stomped to her room.

Drumming his fingers along the smooth oak table, Michael felt the shame sear his heart. Maybe Ma was right. If he out and out asked Star if she had stolen from her guardian, would she admit to it? But if she denied the accusation, how could he ever believe her?

ten

Star slowly roused to the rumble of thunder outside her window. After enduring storms for three days in a row, she was becoming accustomed to nature's way of waking her. She rolled over, buried her face in her pillow, and wished desperately she could sink back into sleep and forget about her dismal life. Instead, she opened her eyes to the wet, gray morning that intruded into her room through the white lacy curtain hanging from the window.

Sunshine might have made facing a new day bearable. As it was, the only things she had to look forward to were rain and mud. . .more loud men and haughty women demanding that she move quicker than humanly possible. . .more insults from Jane. . .more yelling from Joe.

As if the stormy days weren't enough to douse her already drooping spirits, lack of sleep made her eyes feel gritty. Every single inch of her body ached, and she'd have gladly donated a week's salary for thirty more minutes of slumber. But sleep wasn't an option. She had to wash and dress, tidy up her section of the room she shared with Rosemary, eat a bite of breakfast, drop off her laundry with Mrs. Barker for the obscene price of one dollar a week, and get to work.

She'd always worked hard; but after one month of backbreaking, twelve-hour days serving meals at Joe's, she had to admit this was the most difficult task she'd ever undertaken. It might not be so bad if she could discern an end in sight. If she could dream for the future. But her dreams had died with her mother; and the days, months, and years stretched before her in gloomy premonition. There was no Prince Charming. No knight on a white steed. No castle. This was life and, tedious as it might be, she was making an honest, respectable living. Not what she'd choose, if she had a choice, but infinitely preferable to the life she would have faced at Luke's Saloon.

A sigh escaped as Star rolled onto her back and lifted her Bible from the table between her cot and Rosemary's bed. Daily time with the Lord was the only thing Star felt she had to look forward to, and she gave up extra sleep in order to receive that life-sustaining nourishment every morning before she left the comfort and warmth of her bed. She opened up to the Psalms and let the words of a man after God's own heart lead her, comfort her, and draw her into fellowship with her Shepherd.

Thirty minutes later, ready to face the rainy weather, she pushed aside the covers and began the process of preparing for the next fifteen hours.

By noon, Star realized she'd been kidding herself. Thirty minutes alone with God was nowhere near enough to keep from wishing she could slap Jane right across the face.

"Star, you forgot to take Mr. Gabriel his coffee." Jane's haughty accusations never failed to annoy Star. More so now that she realized the girl was trying to humiliate her at every turn. Star had come to the conclusion that Joe's employee problems weren't so much his fault as they were a result of his daughter's nasty disposition.

"I didn't forget to take him the coffee, Jane," she said, forcing herself not to grit her teeth. "I had to take Mr. and Mrs. Arnold their food before it got cold." She refrained from reminding the girl that it wasn't even her job to wait on the Arnolds. As was becoming a habit, Jane neglected her customers shamefully, forcing Star to take care of them. Star wouldn't mind so much if there were a legitimate reason, but it seemed the girl did it purposely so that she could make it appear Star was the one neglecting the restaurant patrons. Star desperately wanted to defend herself, but she was trying hard to heed the Bible's advice to "do good to those who hurt you."

"Well, don't blame me if Mr. Gabriel complains about you to Pa." With that, Jane flounced away.

Gritting her teeth, Star took the coffeepot and headed toward the dining room.

"Star."

She turned, steadying herself for another customer she didn't have enough hands to take care of. Her pulse quickened as she met Michael's gaze. He sat alone at a table in the center of the room. How she had failed to notice him, Star couldn't fathom, but she didn't take time to ponder the question. Her hand went instinctively to her head, and she smoothed back her hair in a futile effort to appear presentable.

"Michael," she said breathlessly. "What are you doing here in the middle of the day?"

"My ax handle busted. Came into town to get another one." He gave her a grin that Star could only describe as devastating. "I thought I'd stop by for a quick hello and a bite of lunch."

And to see me? Star forced the hopeful words from her mind before foolishly voicing them.

"How about my coffee, Miss Star?"

From two tables over, Mr. Gabriel's voice arrested Star's attention. Her cheeks flooded with warmth. "Excuse me a minute, Michael. I'll be right back to get your order."

"Take your time," he said softly.

"I'm sorry, Mr. Gabriel."

The jovial man gave her a broad smile, his attitude far removed from the impatience of a man who might complain to the boss about lack of service. "I hate to begrudge a young man the pleasure of conversing with a beauty such as yourself, but I need my warm cup of coffee on such a miserable day."

Wishing desperately that his voice didn't boom as loudly as the thunder outside, Star poured his coffee.

She turned back to Michael but couldn't quite bring herself to look him in the eye. "What can I get for you?"

He cleared his throat. "You can look at me, first of all."

Reluctantly, she did so.

"How are you?" His voice was so filled with genuine concern, Star couldn't help the tears that sprang to her eyes. She lowered her lashes, but not quickly enough.

"Why don't you come home? Ma can still use someone to help her out with the house and Aimee."

Briefly, she considered his offer—even allowed herself a split-second dream that Michael would fall in love with her, but a bellow from Joe brought her back to reality. "Star, get over here and pick up these orders!"

"I'm sorry, Michael. I have to go. H—have you decided what you'd like to eat?"

With a scowl, he ordered a steak.

Hurrying about her duties, Star didn't have a moment to breathe, let alone continue her disconcerting conversation with Michael. When she saw him rise and glance in her direction, she tried to go to him and say good-bye, but a customer stopped her.

His expression darkened in disappointment. She shrugged and smiled, then lifted her hand in farewell. With a reluctant smile of his own, he returned her wave, then stepped out the door, leaving a cavern in her heart.

"Forget about him." Jane brushed by her and spoke the words for Star's ears only. "He's not worth it. None of them are worth it."

Star finished taking the order, then followed Jane to the kitchen. "I don't know what you're talking about."

The girl snorted. "Don't try to deny being in love with him. It's written plainly on your face."

Star tried to appear nonchalant, but inwardly she groaned at Jane's words. Had she really been that transparent? Grabbing a tray, she filled the order for an impatient couple with twin sons. She remained silent, hoping Jane would let the matter drop, but Jane followed her back into the dining room and continued to bait her. "A man like that will never marry a girl like you."

"Leave it alone, Jane," Star hissed.

True to her pattern, Jane continued in her mocking tone. "With your pretty eyes and smooth skin, you might get a man like that to sweet talk you into being alone with him, but don't fool yourself into thinking he's in love with you. Better for you to take what you can get out of his interest while it lasts."

Star gasped and swung around to face Jane. As she did so, the plates slid from her tray and crashed to the floor. Staring in horror at the clutter, Star knew Jane had finally succeeded in her efforts. Joe appeared from the kitchen and flew into a rage at the mess.

"Clean this up and get out of here. And don't expect to be paid. The wasted food will more than make up for what I owe you this week!"

Incensed, Star drew herself up with as much dignity as she could muster under the watchful gaze of every customer in the place. "I will not clean up a bit of this mess." She glared at Jane. "You can clean it up yourself, you hateful, nasty girl." She hurried to the back, snatched up her bag and shawl, and huffed her way through the dining room.

As she stepped into the muddy street, the only satisfaction Star received was knowing that Jane would have to clean up the mess. By the time she'd walked only a few steps, her conscience seized her, and with a stomp, she spun around and headed back to Joe's.

The dining room buzzed with shocked whispers as she walked back to the mess and knelt down to help Jane clean it up. "There is no way my pa is taking you back."

"I don't expect him to, but it's not right that you should have to clean up a mess I made. Also, I'd like to apologize for calling you a hateful, nasty girl. I was wrong."

The girl gave a short laugh. "Something you learned from that Bible of yours?"

"Yes," she answered, unwilling to be goaded into an argument.

Jane studied her for a second, then scowled. "Anyone in her right mind would have walked out without a second look, especially since you and I both know this wouldn't have happened if I hadn't made you mad."

Surprised by the girl's honesty, Star nodded. "That's true, but I'm not responsible for your actions. . .just mine." She stood and deposited the tray with food and empty tin dishes on a nearby table, then glanced at Jane. "I don't know what I did to make you hate me. I wish we could have worked together. I needed the position. But more than that, I wish I could have convinced you that God loves you, Jane."

"No one can convince me of that. Thank you for coming back to help me clean up, but you'd best get out of here before Pa comes out." She turned, grabbed the tray Star had just set down, and headed back to the kitchen.

With a sigh, Star left Joe's once more, this time knowing she'd done all she could to make things right between herself and Jane.

She stood on the boardwalk and debated whether or not to go to Rosemary's next door. She wasn't ready to share her humiliating experience. Instead, she decided to go to the boardinghouse, get into some dry clothes, and practice sewing the doll dresses she'd been working on for Aimee's birthday. With her mind displaying images of frilly doll things, she stepped heedlessly into the street. She instantly regretted her lack of attention as her boot squished and water rushed in, soaking her stockings. With a groan, she tried to step over the puddle with her other foot, but she overstepped and lost her footing. The ground rose up to meet her in a flash, and she had no chance to regain her balance before plunging headlong into the mud.

≈

Michael's heart nearly stopped as he watched Star fall. He pulled his team up and wrapped the reins around the brake, then hopped down. The sight of her trying to stand and gain her footing melted him. He slipped his way through the mud, nearly losing his own footing. By the time he reached her, she was sitting at the edge of the road looking pitifully dejected. "Let me help you, Honey."

"Oh, Michael." Rather than take his proffered hand, she covered her face with her own. Seeing that she was in no state of mind to be rational, he scooped her up in his arms and carried her to his wagon.

She continued to weep as he set her carefully in the seat and walked around to his own side. He scooted close to her and wrapped her in his arms. "Shhh. Star, don't cry. It's just a little mud. It'll wash off."

"M—Mrs. Barker only allows baths on S—Saturday."

Michael couldn't hold back a chuckle. He squeezed her closer for a second, then let her go. He reached inside his pocket and withdrew his handkerchief.

Star looked from the cloth to his eyes and gave a trembly smile. "Think it'll do any good?"

He laughed. "Probably not."

She took it anyway and dabbed delicately at her pert little nose.

Nearly overcome with a desire to take her into his arms and kiss the quivering from her lips, Michael reached for her. The startled look in her eyes brought him back to his senses. He drew back. "Come on," he said suddenly. "I'll take you to the boardinghouse, and you can pack a small bag."

"What do you mean?"

"Come out to the farm and take a bath and spend the night. I'll bring you back into town early enough to be at work on time."

Her eyes filled once more.

"What is it?"

"Joe fired me." She said the words with such remorse, Michael didn't have the heart to let out the whoop of glee he felt.

"Why did he do that?"

A shrug lifted her shoulders. "I dropped a whole tray of food on the floor."

"You did?"

"Yes."

The clipped answer signaled her desire not to pursue the

matter, so Michael detoured the conversation. "What will you do now?"

A heavy sigh escaped her lips. "I'm not sure. Mrs. Slavens mentioned to Rosemary just a couple of days ago that she would be looking for domestic help before long. Her housemaid is getting married in a month."

Michael tried not to show his exasperation, but he couldn't understand her at all. "Why not come back home and help Ma out if you're going to do domestic work anyway?"

"Because I can't, that's all. If Miss Hannah really needed me, I'd come and attend to household duties and not ask for a penny, but we both know she doesn't. I accepted your generosity long enough. I can't go back. Something will turn up. God won't leave me helpless."

Realizing the matter was settled in her mind, Michael nodded as he pulled the horses to a stop in front of the boardinghouse. "Then how about coming to the farm anyway? Ma and Aimee have missed you something awful." He refrained from admitting his own feelings about her absence. There was no reason to lead her on when he could never marry her, though his traitorous heart wanted nothing more than to ask to court her and explore the possibility that she might be the woman for him. No matter how attracted he was to her lovely face and sweet spirit, there was no getting around the fact that she had stolen from her guardian and apparently hadn't the faintest intention of confessing. How could he overlook the dishonesty when she would be teaching and training his daughter? He walked around to her side of the wagon and reached for her.

Swallowing past a lump in his throat, he tried to still his racing heart as she slid effortlessly into his arms. "So what do you say? Will you come for a visit? I'll bring you back tomorrow." Unless Ma could somehow talk her into staying.

Star smiled through her mud-caked face and nodded. "All right. Give me ten minutes to gather my things."

He started to follow her, but she touched his arm, bringing him to a stop. "You'd best wait out here. Mrs. Barker doesn't like men callers in the house as it is and, considering my appearance, I'll have enough explaining to do."

Patting her hand, he smiled. "I'll wait in the wagon." As rain dripped from the brim of his hat, he started to have second thoughts about taking Star to the farm. As soaked through as she already was, she should probably stay inside rather than coming back out in this weather. He hated the thought of taking a chance that she might get sick and was just about to go and suggest she stay at the boardinghouse when she appeared—still in her wet gown, though she'd replaced her wet shawl with a dry one.

"Why didn't you change your dress?" he asked, as he helped her into the wagon.

A faint blush stained her cheeks. "My other dress is being laundered. I didn't want to wear the pretty ones until I get the mud off."

"Makes sense." He climbed into his seat and grabbed the reins. Cutting her a sideways glance, he snatched his hat from his head and set it on hers.

"What are you doing?"

"Protecting your head from the rain."

"I can't take your hat. You might get sick."

"I'll take the risk." He smiled at her look of worry. "Ma's going to have plenty to say to me as it is about the condition you're in."

She dropped her gaze to her fingers. The large hat covered her face, and he almost snatched it back so he could see her. "My muddy clothes aren't your fault. You rescued me."

For the first time, Michael realized Star felt the spark between them every bit as much as he did. She must wonder why he hadn't acted on it. He cleared his throat. "Listen, Star. . ."

She lifted her head, her wide, beautiful eyes waiting expectantly. "Yes?"

"I know you said before that you didn't want to discuss your past, but if there's anything you'd like to. . ." He shifted his gaze back to the horses as a frown creased her brow.

"Like to what?" she asked, her voice trembling.

"If you have something weighing heavy on your heart, I'll listen. The Bible says to confess our faults to one another."

She straightened her shoulders. "Well, how about you? If there are any faults you'd like to confess, I'd be happy to hear them."

Indignation swelled his chest. "Me?"

"Or don't you have any faults?" She was baiting him. Michael knew it and still couldn't keep from walking right into her trap.

"Of course I have faults. . . . Everybody has—"

"Then let's hear them." She folded her arms across her chest and waited.

"I'm not going to sit here and tell you all my faults."

"No?" She sniffed. "But the Bible says to confess them."

"I know what the Bible says," he growled, irritated by the twist of events.

"Then it doesn't apply to you?"

"Just drop it, all right? I'm sorry I tried to help."

Silence hung in the air, thicker than the fog rolling in, and remained between them until the house came into view.

"I don't know what you think I've done, Michael," Star said in a small voice, "but I don't want to think about the past. Your daughter was the one who taught me that our sins are thrown far away when we repent. If God doesn't remember the things I've done, why should I bring them up, and why should you worry about them?"

Her words sifted the irritation from Michael. He had his own past he'd like to forget. He nodded. "I won't bring it up again."

"Thank you."

He drew the wagon to a halt, and Star hopped down as the door flew open, effectively halting any chance he had to make an apology. Aimee ran out the door and into Star's arms before anyone could stop her.

"How come you're all dirty?" the little girl asked when she finally let Star go.

"I fell in the mud again. Can you believe that? And look—now you're all dirty too."

Aimee shrugged. "I like it."

A giggle escaped Star's lips and reached Michael's ears like an angel's song. Contentment flooded him.

"Star!" Ma said from the doorway, her face beaming with unabashed joy. "Just look at you! Get in here so we can dry you off before you catch your death!"

Michael lifted her bag from the back of the wagon and watched as Star fell into his mother's arms.

Star was home. The only question was. . .how could he convince her to stay?

eleven

Star had almost forgotten how wonderful it was to be at the Riley farm, to be fussed over by Miss Hannah. . .and admired by Aimee.

And just to be in the same room with Michael. . . Her heart had felt his absence every aching moment of each day and night during the past month. Now it soared with a joy that made her feel downright giddy.

She was grateful that the steady rain kept him hovering in the cabin, getting underfoot as she and Miss Hannah prepared dinner. The cabin echoed with the sounds of Aimee's gleeful laughter. She sat on the floor next to the fire, squeezing rags soaked with milk into the greedy mouths of five whining puppies.

According to the little girl, Mrs. Paxter from the next farm over had hotfooted it to the front door with a wiggling burlap bag in her hands. Without so much as a howdy-do, the woman had declared poor Cannonball a pa.

Michael chuckled at his daughter's telling of the story. "And Ma took every single one of them in just like she's a grammy again."

Miss Hannah rolled her eyes and shrugged at Star. "That cold-hearted Paxter woman threatened to toss the whole bag of them into the creek. Aimee let up a howl louder than an Indian war cry. What was I to do?"

Star's gaze went to Michael, and they exchanged knowing grins. They both knew Miss Hannah wouldn't have let anyone harm even one of the furry little bothers, war cry or no war cry.

Looking from one to the other, Miss Hannah let out a "harrumph" and propped her hands on her hips. "Aimee, go wash up and come to the table."

Star would have followed her into the kitchen, but Miss Hannah motioned her away. "You sit down. I'll have everything out here in a jiffy. You too, Michael. Sit and keep Star company until dinner's on the table."

Tingles raced up Star's spine as Michael's arm brushed hers when he pulled out the chair for her to sit down. He lingered just a bit longer than necessary, and Star inhaled the combined smells of soap and wood smoke. His closeness sent her heart racing. She closed her eyes as he stood behind her chair, his hand gripping her arm.

"Star. . ." His husky whisper weakened her knees, and she was glad to be sitting; otherwise she feared her legs might not have held her. He crouched down next to her. His gaze flickered over her face and settled on her lips. But just when she thought he would lean in and kiss her, he seemed to gather his wits and looked her in the eye.

Scarcely able to breath, Star waited for him to speak.

"Pa! Are they clean enough to eat?" Aimee bounded into the room and shoved her palms between Star and Michael, effectively halting conversation or anything else that might have occurred between them.

A wry grin tipped Michael's lips. He grabbed both of his daughter's dimpled hands and appeared to examine them. "Hmmm. They *do* look clean enough to eat." With that, he brought them to his lips and pretended to devour the little fingers. Aimee giggled uncontrollably and infectiously until Star was giggling right along with her.

Miss Hannah bustled through the kitchen with a pot in her hands. She sent Michael and Aimee an affectionate smile as she set dinner on the table. "All right. Stop the shenanigans, and let's eat before the food gets cold."

Michael held her hand during the blessing, as he had many times before. This time, however, he didn't let it go immediately upon saying "Amen." Star glanced up in surprise. He held her fast with his beautiful, brown-eyed gaze.

His thumb caressed the back of her hand, sending physical and emotional sensations throughout her being.

After a quick glance at his mother, then at Aimee, he focused his full attention upon Star. Her throat went dry, and she couldn't have looked away if a herd of buffalo had stampeded through the room.

"Michael?"

"I need to ask you something," he began.

Star's pulse thudded in her ears.

"Can we eat?" Obviously sensing the intensity of the moment, Aimee voiced the question with a loud whisper.

"Shhhh," Miss Hannah scolded.

"It's all right, Ma."

Star's stomach turned in disappointment, but she could no more have been annoyed with the charming little girl than she could have denied her love for Michael.

"Aimee, can you wait just a few minutes before eating so I can ask Miss Star a question?"

Here? In front of everyone?

"I can wait, Pa."

Star's cheeks burned under Miss Hannah's watchful gaze. The woman's eyes glistened with unshed tears, and she gave a suspicious sniff. "Go on, then, and spit it out. Supper's just sitting here getting cold as December."

"All right," Michael took both of Star's hands. "I wanted Ma and Aimee here for this because they're part of my life and deserve a say so."

Star nodded. So far, he hadn't said much of anything.

"It's no secret that I have reservations about the things you've held back—your past and all." He smiled, adding to Star's relief and confusion. "But you were right earlier when you said God doesn't hold your past against you. I believe you've given Him your entire heart. At least it seems so. I hope some day you'll trust me enough to share that part of your life with me."

"Michael. . ." Oh, how she wished she could tell him everything. What a comfort it would be to unburden herself and cry on his shoulder about Mama's death at Luke's hands. But every time she'd almost opened up over the weeks she lived at the farm, and most recently to Rosemary, she remembered Luke's biting words. "What decent man will want her when he finds out what she is?"

Michael pressed her hand. "It's all right. You don't have to share for now. I just wanted you to know that I'm here, and when you're ready, you can tell me anything or nothing. It's your choice."

Star's lips curved into a tender smile. "Thank you, Michael."

"Land sakes. Get on with the askin'!"

A scowl marred Michael's handsome face, but Star couldn't help but agree with Miss Hannah. Her palms were becoming damp in Michael's grasp, and her heart felt about to race from her chest.

He gathered a long, agonizingly slow breath and fixed her with his gaze. "I want to know if you'll. . ."

Yes, yes, yes!

". . .allow me to come courting."

A loud snort from Miss Hannah echoed Star's feelings. Star lowered her gaze in an effort to mask her disappointment with the appearance of demure consideration of his question.

"Pa wants to court Miss Star. Does that mean they're getting married?" Aimee's loud whisper, obviously meant for Miss Hannah, brought a rush of heat to Star's cheeks.

Venturing a peek at Michael, she noticed the look of stunned revelation in his eyes. His own face went red. He cleared his throat and let go of her hands to take a drink of water. "Uh—Star, it seems. . ."

Awash with sympathy for the misunderstood man, Star smiled and pressed his hand. His eyes widened with renewed hope. "I'd be pleased to accept your offer of a courtship. Thank you for asking me."

"Well, then," Miss Hannah's boisterous voice broke through before Michael could come up with an answer. "That *little* matter is settled. So how about we eat before Aimee wastes away to skin and bone."

During dinner, Star savored every single bite of the chicken and dumplings. For dessert, Miss Hannah produced a fluffy white cake, fit for a king. Indeed, Star felt like an honored guest, and more so, now that Michael was officially courting her.

In the morning, they said very little, trying to act as naturally as possible during breakfast. Conversation during the ride into town bordered on the ridiculous, and Star grew impatient as she responded to observations about the weather—which had finally cleared up—for the third time. Still, she felt she had to ask the question that had been burning in her since his question the night before. She practiced what to say in her mind for the last mile of the ride into town, missing most of Michael's not-so-fascinating tale of last year's rainy weather.

"Michael," she finally blurted, when they reached the boardinghouse and he helped her from the wagon. "What does courting mean, exactly? Wh—what do we do?"

An incredulous smile tipped the corners of his lips. "No young man's ever come calling on you before?" He released her and grabbed her bag from the back of the wagon.

She shook her head.

He offered her his arm, but she hesitated. "What about Mrs. Barker?"

"She'd better get used to me." He sent her a wink and tweaked her nose. "I'm going to see my girl safely inside every time I drop her off from now on."

Star's stomach turned over at the meaningful smile. She tucked her hand in the crook of his arm and held her head high.

"To answer your question," he said, pausing at the step, "courting means I'll escort you to services on Sunday, we'll have picnics together and go to socials and dances. You will come for dinner as often as possible. In other words, we are getting ready for the possibility of a future together."

The images his words invoked filled Star with such hope, she didn't have the heart to tell him that if she didn't find another position soon, her money would run out and she'd be forced to leave Hobbs. She pushed the grim thought from her mind and sent him her best smile. "Then I suppose you'll be escorting me to the box social next week?" The bazaar the month before had been such a success, the ladies society had organized a box social to raise money for a church bell.

He chuckled. "The gentleman's supposed to do the asking."

"After the hard time you had asking if you could come calling, I'm afraid asking anyone anything doesn't seem to be your gift." She gave him a teasing grin. "I thought I'd save us the time and trouble by bringing it up myself."

"About asking you to court instead of what Aimee said. . ." His face reddened. "I just—"

"Michael, you don't have to explain. I was—am happy that you think I'm good enough for you to come calling on me. If you decide in the future that you made a mistake. . .well, better that mistake is one you can fix."

The intensity on his face as he looked into her eyes nearly melted Star's legs into a puddle. "You humble me, Star," he said, his voice soft and filled with emotion.

The door opened suddenly, causing Star to jump. "Mrs. Barker," she said into the scowling face. "You nearly scared the life out of me."

"What are you two doing, standing out here in broad daylight?"

Michael went rigid. Star pressed his arm, hoping to thwart any comment he might feel compelled to make in their defense.

"Mr. Riley was kind enough to carry my bag to the door." Star turned to Michael, silently pleading with him not to offend her landlady.

He handed over the bag and tipped his hat. "I'll see you soon, Star. Good day, Mrs. Barker."

"Good day, Mr. Riley," the landlady returned, and Star caught a glimpse of amusement in her eyes.

"Mrs. Barker?"

The elderly lady laughed and opened the door wider to give Star room to walk through. She squeezed Star's shoulder. "He certainly is a good catch, young lady. I don't imagine I'll be able to keep him out of the parlor much longer, will I?"

A giggle burst from Star's lips. "No, Ma'am."

"It's just as well you'll have a man like Michael Riley looking out for you. That Joe is here to see you."

"Joe? From the restaurant?"

With a frown, Mrs. Barker waved toward the kitchen. "Who else? He's in there. Probably intending to beg you to go back to that disgraceful place."

"Oh, I hope so," Star said quickly. "I have to work if I'm to continue to pay rent, Mrs. Barker."

An indulgent smile curved the older woman's thin lips. "I suppose you're right."

To Star's amazement, Joe did ask her to come back. Within an hour, she was back at work. She floated through the day, despite the demanding customers, Joe's grumbling, and Jane's sulking. The girl seemed to have mellowed a bit, and Star hoped she had put aside her dislike. Regardless, God had a reason for sending Star back. Her work here wasn't finished, and she prayed Jane would give her a chance to show her Christ's love.

❧

"Star will be ready in a few minutes," Mrs. Barker said regally. "She asked me to inform you that Joe held the restaurant open a little later than promised, and she is running behind. You may sit in the parlor and wait."

"Thank you." Michael groaned every time he thought about Star going back to that restaurant to work. Better that she'd taken the position as housekeeper for Mrs. Slavens. Working for the woman couldn't be any worse than working for Joe. But Star was firm in her decision, believing God had sent her back for Joe's daughter. The fact that Ma agreed with Star irked him. He had hoped to persuade her to come back to the farm for good, but even Ma balked at the idea.

"You know how folks talk." With her hands on her hips, she'd looked at him with a disgusted frown. "Now, if you had asked the *right* question the other night and made short work of the engagement, things would be a little different now, and Star wouldn't have to go back to that place."

He had no defense against Ma's argument. She was right, but Michael couldn't quite bring himself to make the commitment of marriage without more assurance that Star would be content to be a wife and mother and that she wouldn't bring trouble into his life like Sarah had. He wanted to trust Star, wanted to release the lock he'd placed upon his heart, but for now, it was better to play it safe.

With a conscious effort, he was attempting to stop comparing her with his late wife, but at times it wasn't easy. Like Sarah, Star was beautiful. Breathtakingly so, though there was a gentleness, a sweetness about Star that Sarah hadn't possessed. But what Clem had told him about her stealing from her guardian only served to strengthen the similarity between the only two women he'd ever loved.

"Michael?" At the sound of Star's breathy voice, he stood and turned toward the door. The sight of her caused a sudden lump in his throat, and he swallowed hard.

Her beautiful violet eyes stood out more than usual in the blue dress she wore. Her mahogany hair hung in curls about her shoulders and was held back with a ribbon to match her gown. "You're a vision," he said when finally able to speak.

A beguiling blush stained her cheeks. "Thank you," she whispered. "You're very handsome yourself, tonight."

She'd seen him in the same Sunday suit every week since she'd known him, but the sincerity in her voice couldn't be denied. He took her hand and brought it to his lips. "Shall we go?"

Once outside, he headed for the wagon, but Star hung back and tugged at his arm. "Let's walk to the church. It's not far."

"Are you sure? The night air's a bit nippy."

Tucking her hand inside the crook of his arm, she tilted her head and dazzled him with a smile. "I'm plenty warm."

Unable to deny her something she obviously wanted to do, he covered her hand with his free one and returned her smile. "Then, let's go."

They walked in companionable silence, and Michael barely noticed the chilly air. He felt nearly uncontainable joy to know that, for the next couple of hours, he had the pleasure of her company and soon everyone would know they were courting. This pleased him on a couple of levels. For one thing, every desperate female between sixteen and thirty-five would know he was calling on Star. And two, the young men constantly vying for Star's attention would also know that fact as well. Then it occurred to him, they were going to a box social and Star had no box. How was he going to know which one was hers?

"Where's your box?"

"What? Oh, you mean for the social?"

"Yes."

"Rosemary took it to the church earlier so that you wouldn't know which one it was."

"But that's not fair. How will I know which box to bid on?"

"That's the whole fun of a box social! Isn't it wonderful? Rosemary says no one is supposed to know and you just end up eating dinner with whomever buys your box."

"You act like you've never been to a box social before."

"I haven't." She giggled. "I wonder who will buy mine."

Enchanted by her playfulness, Michael pulled her aside, into the shadow of the feed store awning. He didn't realize he intended to kiss her until suddenly she was looking up at him, her face bathed in the lamplight, eyes shining in wonder. He slid his hands up her arms and lightly rested them on her neck. Drawing a quick, shallow breath, he traced the line of her jaw with both thumbs, his fingers laced in locks of silken tresses.

"Star," he breathed, just before closing his lips over hers. She responded clumsily at first; and, delighted, Michael knew she'd never been kissed. The realization only made him desire her more, and he gathered her closer. She melded against him and wrapped her arms around his neck.

Dizzy with the feel of her in his arms, the sweetness of her surrender to his kisses, Michael almost lost all sense of reason and begged her to become his wife. He might have, if she hadn't pulled away just then, released a soft sigh, and rested her head gently against his chest. His heart pounded and he knew she must hear her name on every beat; but the trusting nature of the simple movement cooled his passion and evoked such tenderness within his breast, he laid his cheek against her hair and closed his eyes, willing his heart to return to normal.

"We better get to the social, or someone will buy your box and I won't be there to punch him in the nose."

She glanced up at him and smiled shyly. "All right."

He tucked her hand in the crook of his arm once more. "Unless of course you want to tell me what to look for. In which case, I won't have to beat anyone up and steal your box away."

"No, Sir. You'll just have to be a good sport."

Raucous laughter blended with the sound of rowdy music coming from the saloon up ahead. A man stumbled outside, accompanied by a lady of the evening.

Michael scowled. "Let's cross the street."

"Why?"

"Because I don't want you that close to the trash up ahead."

Star stopped dead in her tracks and stared at him with disbelief. Her lips trembled. "God doesn't make trash."

"Maybe not, but someone does, and I'd just as soon not have you exposed to it."

"Is it me you don't want exposed to it, Michael, or you?" She stomped indignantly and walked past him.

Reaching out, he snagged her upper arm and stopped her. She wheeled around to face him, anger sparkling in her eyes. "Turn me loose this instant!"

"Lower your voice, please." Michael couldn't understand why he'd offended her, but it was obvious she would fight to have her say.

"I refuse to cross the street as though these people are somehow not as good as I. Jesus died for that poor woman's sins every bit as much as He did for mine."

"That may be," he replied through gritted teeth and righteous indignation, "but you aren't living in *that* sin. You have asked forgiveness for anything you did in the past and are living a respectable life."

"You don't know her! Maybe she has no choice. Maybe she needs help." She shook her head in disgust. "If the good, *respectable* folks of Hobbs would give women like that a chance, maybe they could change their lives, raise their daughters in a little house somewhere, and go to church without feeling like society's *trash*. Ever think of that?"

"Star. . ." She just didn't understand that women such as this one couldn't change who they were. Sarah never could.

"Don't! I'll not have you escort me to the social. You can't miss my box. I used the fabric left over from making this dress to decorate it. I wanted to surprise you and make it easy for you to figure out which was mine. But I will thank you *not* to do any bidding for my box tonight." With that she spun around and walked along the boardwalk, her heels clacking with every step. Michael bristled when she smiled at the lady of the evening as she passed. "Lovely night, isn't it? I'm so happy the rain has stopped."

The woman and man gaped after her. Then the woman turned, as though to head back inside. Michael drew in a breath at the pensive look that covered her face. But when she caught him staring at her, her eyebrows drew up and her lips curved into a sensual smile.

Disgusted, he looked away and crossed the street. *Lie down with pigs, rise up dirty and stinking of the same filth as the animals.* He'd gone that route before and had no intention of ever doing it again, nor would he allow any woman he married to voice such opinions and become fodder for speculation and gossip. If Star was to be his wife, she'd have to learn to keep to her own side of the street.

One question burned in his mind. . . . On which side did she belong?

twelve

Star's heart raced when Reverend Hank, acting as auctioneer, held up her box for display.

Michael stepped forward, poised for action. Star slammed her hands on her hips. Clearly he hadn't taken her seriously when she'd told him not to bid on her box. Well, he wouldn't get away with it. She'd sooner eat with a skunk.

"Now, this is lovely," Hank called. "And if I'm not mistaken, I smell fried chicken, fresh bread." He lifted the cover ever so slightly, then looked over the room, a wide grin on his face. "Mmm. . .and apple pie. A meal fit for a king. Who wants to start the bidding?"

Michael glanced at her, and Star sent him the full force of her glare. With a scowl, he turned toward his brother. "Fifty cents."

Hank's lips twitched into a smirk, and he looked across the room. "Fifty cents? Are you young men going to let this delicious meal go for only fifty cents? Just smelling this wonderful aroma has my stomach grumbling something fierce. I'm awfully tempted to bid on it myself."

"All right. Fifty-five cents." Michael's annoyed voice filled the room, and suddenly the place roared with laughter. Star covered her mouth with her hand to suppress her own mirth.

Michael's face flooded with color at the realization that he'd just upped his own bid. He looked around with a sheepish grin and shrugged. "I'm partial to apple pie."

"Sixty cents!" Star turned to see Joe had placed a bid for her box. And then it began. From all over the room, bids of a nickel more each came in, raising the price until, at two dollars, most of the men dropped out, including Joe. Michael and Mr. Cole, a lean farmer who ate frequently at the restaurant, seemed to be warring for the box. Hank glanced at her and winked. Star's eyes widened. He knew it was hers! Did that mean Mr. Cole knew too? Or was it just a coincidence that he kept trying to outbid Michael?

"Looks like Michael is going to have some competition from now on." Star turned at the sound of Rosemary's voice.

"But how did Mr. Cole know the box was mine?"

"Besides the fact that it matches your dress?" Rosemary's teasing laugh was infectious.

Star giggled. "I didn't want to take any chances that Michael wouldn't figure out which one was mine."

"A stroke of genius!" Rosemary looped her arm through Star's and glanced toward the men. "The bid is up to three dollars. Who do you think will win?"

"From the look on Michael's face, I don't think he'll let it go, short of mortgaging the farm."

Rosemary threw back her head and laughed. "I think you may be right. But Mr. Cole looks pretty determined as well. I've noticed he spends a lot of time staring at you during services."

Dismissing Rosemary's observation with a wave, Star sniffed. "I wouldn't want a man who can't pay attention in church."

Glancing about, Star found plenty of eyes focused on her. Apparently everyone had figured out that the box was hers, and clearly they were tired of the bidding war. Everyone, it seemed, wanted to get on with the auction. Everyone, that was, except for, perhaps, the members of the ladies society who were no doubt hearing the lovely ringing of a new bell.

Stepping forward, Star released an exasperated breath. "I'm going to put a stop to this."

Rosemary grabbed her arm. "Wait. Let them drive the bidding price a little higher. They can both afford it, and bells aren't cheap." She gave a teasing grin. "Just a couple of dollars more?"

"Seven dollars!" Michael's steady, determined voice rang out. The man had lost his mind! Seven dollars for a boxed dinner that, truth be told, Rosemary had cooked while Star worked at Joe's. The only thing Star had been responsible for was the decorating. She'd done none of the cooking.

"Seven fifty!" Mr. Cole called out, his voice just as determined as Michael's.

Star managed to capture Michael's gaze. She silently pleaded with him to stop the humiliating event. The intensity of his returning stare sizzled the air between them, and Star knew he was remembering the kiss they'd shared, just as she was doing.

"Seven fifty?" Obviously, Hank could barely contain himself, so amused was he by Michael's competition. "Going once. . ."

Michael's eyes went wide, and he snapped to attention. "Hey, I'm not finished! Eight dollars."

"Eight fifty." Mr. Cole stepped next to Michael, clearly challenging him. Michael's eyes narrowed, and his jaw muscle jumped as he clenched and unclenched his teeth. "Ten dollars!" he called.

Rosemary chuckled. "Ten dollars is a big help toward the bell. Be my guest at putting a stop to this battle before everyone starves to death."

Star nodded. Stomping to the front of the room, she stood before them both. "This is ridiculous," she said, including both in her glare. "You're embarrassing me and making spectacles of yourselves."

"I'll risk the humiliation for dinner with you, Miss Star," Mr. Cole said, grinning at her.

"That's very sweet of you, Mr. Cole."

"Call me Thomas."

"No, thank you. The fact is that Michael and I are courting." She bristled at the look of triumph on Michael's face. "Although I'm mad as a wet hen at him right now, and I have no intention of eating with him even if he spends a hundred dollars on that cold chicken."

"You two are courting, for sure?" Thomas asked, looking from one to the other.

"Yes," Star replied. "So don't waste your money if you're hoping for anything more than dinner. I won't accept anyone else as a suitor."

Extending his hand to Michael, the farmer grinned. "Looks like you got yourself a ten-dollar meal, Riley. You're a lucky fellow." He turned to the room and put up his hands in surrender. "The lady has convinced me to concede. Preacher, bring out the next box, and maybe I can find another dinner companion to help mend my wounded pride."

"That's the spirit, Cole," Hank said. Through a smattering of laughter and congratulations to Michael, Hank handed over the box. He patted his brother's shoulder and grabbed the next one in line. "Mmm. . .what a surprise. This one smells like fried chicken and fresh bread too."

Michael turned to Star. "Come on, I need to talk to you."

Folding her arms across her chest, Star jerked her chin. "I refuse to eat with you. You just wasted your hard-earned dollars."

"Ten minutes?" he asked, his lips close to her ear. He took her by the elbow, the warmth of his hand and tickle of his breath making her knees go weak.

"F–fine. Ten minutes. But that's all."

They looked around for a quiet spot, but with the bidding and laughter going on, there was none to be had. "Do you mind going outside?" Michael asked. "I know it's a little chilly."

"It's not so bad," Star replied. "Just let me grab my shawl."

Michael stepped back and allowed Star to walk outside ahead of him. "How about walking back to the boarding-house and eating this in the kitchen?"

So much for only giving him ten minutes, but her curiosity got the better of her. "All right. I'm sure Mrs. Barker won't object as long as I clean up any mess we make. There will be plenty of chaperones in the house."

With a bit of annoyance, she noticed he led her to the

opposite side of the street so they wouldn't have to walk past the saloon. She remained silent, and so did he. The last hour, she'd felt his presence as strongly as if he'd been next to her, although in truth, she'd avoided him. Hearing him call the saloon girl trash had been more than she could overlook without speaking out. Her heart ached at the thought that one day in the past, he might have been talking about her own mother—her mother, who had felt she had no choice but to stay in that life. Luke had convinced her that she couldn't raise Star without his help. But Star knew they would have been all right if they'd moved somewhere away from the mining and lumber camps. Somewhere folks wouldn't be likely to recognize them.

When the music from the saloon across the street reached them, Star ventured a peek at Michael. "There are always two sides to any story, you know."

He slipped his arm about her shoulders and drew her close as they continued to walk. "I know, Honey." His gentle endearment and protective gesture sent shivers up her spine and soothed her troubled thoughts. Maybe things would be all right between them, after all.

Once they were clear of the saloon, Michael tightened his hold, and they crossed the street. "I need to explain my side of the story. I know it seems that I'm unusually harsh. But I have to be. That life is the most abominable I can imagine."

He gathered a shaky breath and stopped walking just before they climbed the boardinghouse steps. He removed his arm from around her and took her hand in one of his. "Can we sit out here for a few minutes? I'd rather not discuss this where folks might hear."

Dread clenched Star's stomach. She nodded, and they sat on the step. Michael set the boxed lunch on the landing behind them. Shifting so that they nearly faced, he drew another deep breath. "First, I'm sorry I was so abrupt with you earlier."

"I forgive you, Michael," she said softly, taken aback by the seriousness of his demeanor. She braced herself. Would he tell her he realized she wasn't the woman for him? Maybe their argument earlier had convinced him that she could never be good enough for him. Although, the fact of the matter was that he knew nothing of her life. He didn't know why Clem had been chasing her or why Luke wanted her back. It wasn't possible that he knew about her mother or that Luke wanted her to work the men at the saloon. Gathering a deep breath, she tried to calm herself. She gave him a nod of encouragement.

"I want to tell you about Aimee's mother."

So, that was it. He had realized he could never love her the way he'd loved his Sarah. She would never measure up to the woman he'd practically enshrined. The woman whose Bible he'd given to Star. The pain clouding his features bespoke his reluctance to hurt her, and she didn't have the heart to let him. She reached forward with her free hand and pressed her fingers to his lips.

"It's all right, Michael. You don't have to tell me. I don't want you to. I don't need to know about Sarah to understand why you can never love the likes of me."

A frown creased his brow, and he took her hand in his, kissed it hard, then pressed it to his chest. "That's not it. I could easily love you, but we can't take this relationship forward until you understand why I feel so strongly about things being right and proper."

There was that word. . . . Star couldn't think of any word more disconcerting than "proper." Unless it was "respectable."

"You have to understand," he went on, "why I hate places like that saloon and why I don't want my family anywhere near those people."

Those people. Star inwardly retreated. She had to tell him the truth. But if she did, she'd lose him. Her heart cried out to God. *Why did You allow me to fall in love with a man who will never love me once he finds out where I come from? Oh, Lord, help me trust You with my heart.*

"Star, my wife was one of those women before I married her."

A gasp escaped Star's lips, and she felt the blood drain from her cheeks.

"I took Sarah out of a house like that."

"Y—you used to go visit the saloon girls?"

"Wha—? Oh, of course not. Never! I was walking past the saloon one morning when I saw her. She was hurt. I found her crying and couldn't pass her by. She was so lovely and fragile. I just. . ." He glanced at Star and shrugged, shaking his head. "I fell in love with her at first sight."

A twinge of jealousy pinched at Star, but she forced it away.

"She convinced me that she wanted to leave that life. She knew all the right things to say. Her pa was a preacher. As she grew up, he'd beaten her every day, until she ran from him. When she went to work for the man who owned the saloon, she figured it couldn't be any worse than the daily beatings. By the time I met her, she'd been a saloon girl for nearly two years."

Tears burned Star's eyes. She'd heard that story—or a form of it—over and over.

"Don't you see, Michael? Not one little girl is born with a desire to grow up and become a prostitute. We all dream of marrying our handsome prince and raising babies, taking care of a home. Circumstances force many young girls into such a life. They don't want it, don't plan it, but it happens. We can't turn our backs on them. Can't treat them as though they have less worth than we do just because we were blessed to escape."

His eyes flicked quickly to hers. "Escape?"

Her impassioned pleas fell silent, and she lowered her gaze, afraid she might let slip more than she felt ready to reveal. "Anyone who grows up in a loving home and isn't forced into that life has escaped it."

"But I rescued Sarah. Or at least I tried to." He released a short, bitter laugh. "She never returned to that place. I bought her new clothes and married her before I'd known her three hours. I adored her. I thought she loved me too; but before long, I realized that I was only a means to an end for her. She'd never intended to stay with me in the first place. She only used me to escape the man who owned the saloon. He'd taken to beating her, and she'd determined to do whatever it took to get away. When she found out she was carrying Aimee, she flew into a rage. I had to practically sit on her for nine months to keep her from doing something to harm the child she carried." He drew a sharp breath. "I'm sorry, I shouldn't have told you that part."

Sickened by surfacing images long stored in the recesses of her memory, Star nodded. She knew of the dangerous measures the girls often took to lose their babies. She thanked God her own mother hadn't done that. "It's all right, go on."

"She kept telling me she was leaving as soon as the baby was born. I prayed. Oh, how I prayed she would change her mind. By that time, my illusions were over. I knew she'd never cared about me, and I certainly didn't find much to love about her. We had the baby to think of, and I couldn't bear the thought of Aimee growing up without a ma. I honestly believed motherhood might change Sarah. Or maybe I just hoped."

"She died giving birth to Aimee?" she asked softly, knowing he was emotionally drained from the discourse, but that he needed to end the tale.

He nodded.

Star pressed her hand against his cheek. "Michael, I understand why you feel as you do, but you have to understand that Sarah was only one hurting soul. There are so many hurting people in this world—people you wouldn't consider suitable company. But all of them need the love of Jesus. We can't turn our backs and treat them as though they have no value, as though association with them might stain us. That's not the way Jesus treated people while He walked the earth. We're His hands, His voice. I was reading a story in the Bible about a woman Jesus met at a well. She had been married many times and was living in sin with a man by the time she encountered Jesus. He didn't use her past against her, Michael. He forgave her. He offered her a drink from the well of life."

"What about the ones who won't accept what Jesus offers?"

"Not all will accept, but it's worth the risk of showing you care, even if you can only save one."

"I couldn't save Sarah. She died without ever seeing our daughter or accepting Christ."

"So the reason you didn't like me wearing her things wasn't because you couldn't bear to see another woman in the clothes of the woman you loved?"

"No," he answered abruptly. His gaze met hers, but he didn't speak.

Hit by realization, Star gasped. "Wearing her tight, low-cut gown made me look like her?"

"Something like that." He averted his gaze.

"You thought I looked too much like a saloon girl, and it made you think I'm like her on the inside. Oh, Michael, you've known the Lord all of your life. When will you understand that it's not what a person wears or how they look that matters to God? I may not have been a Christian as long as you have, Michael, but I've discovered that God looks on the heart. Just because I wore her clothes doesn't make me like Sarah."

"I know that now. But I have to be careful. I don't want Aimee hurt. I have to make certain the woman I invite into our lives is someone respectable, someone who won't shame us."

"Is that what you're afraid I'll do?"

The look he gave her melted her defenses. His lips curved into a hint of a smile, then he lifted her hand to his lips and pressed a kiss to her fingers. "I'm falling in love with you."

The joy Star should have felt at his revelation was sucked from her by his next words. "But I fell in love with Sarah. I believed everything she told me about wanting to change, and I married her. A woman like that! I still can't believe it. Not that I regret having Aimee, but how could I have been so foolish?"

He was afraid she was like Sarah—and she might have been, if Luke had had his way. Star shuddered. Suddenly unable to look him in the eye, she glanced down. Michael would never accept where she'd come from. She made a decision at the same moment she stood. "Michael, thank you for telling me about Sarah. It did help me to understand your reaction tonight. I—I'm sorry, but I don't think it's a good idea for us to continue courting."

"Why?" Michael stood and grasped her arm. "Star, I care about you. I don't want to lose you."

Tears stung her eyes and her chin quivered. "There is something you don't know about me. Something I don't believe you could accept."

"What?" He tightened his hold on her arms. "Tell me who you were before you came to live with us at the farm. Who is your family? You mentioned your mother passed on, but what about your pa? Brothers and sisters? Grandparents?"

Star hesitated a minute and honestly considered it. She even imagined herself pouring it all out to him. All about Mama, Samson and Lila, about Luke. But when one person knew a secret, somehow others learned of it. She knew Michael wouldn't purposely gossip, but things like that had a way of spreading. She couldn't bear the thought of people looking upon her with disdain, folks never looking her in the eye, ladies grabbing their children and crossing the street rather than being forced to share a boardwalk with her.

"Please, Michael. Just leave it alone and respect my decision. As I've said before, there are things you don't know about me. Things that would change how you feel."

"Nothing would do that."

He tried to pull her to him, but she jerked away and hurriedly opened the door. "Don't come calling. I won't see you."

"Wait," he said just before she could close the door. "I know about Luke."

Star's heart nearly stopped. "You do?" she asked in a hoarse whisper.

"Clem told me that you stole some money. I was waiting for you to confess it to me, but I understand if you can't. The important thing is that you have asked God for forgiveness. We can make things right with your guardian later."

"With my what?" Michael believed her to be a thief? Despair congealed with indignation, and she shook her head. "Michael, just forget about it. You don't know what you think you know." The last thing she saw when she shut the door was his look of utter disbelief.

She didn't blame him. She was finding it difficult to wrap her mind around tonight's turn of events as well.

Tears stung her eyes and flowed down her cheeks.

She trudged up the steps to the room she shared with Rosemary. After changing into her nightgown, she picked up her Bible, hoping to find answers or at least comfort. But the words ran together, and nothing penetrated her aching heart. Finally, she gathered a long breath and set the book on the table. Snuggling under the covers, she stared at the ceiling as though the wood slats above her might bring answers. She couldn't quite bring herself to reach beyond the ceiling in her heart, knowing she should have been honest in the beginning and trusted God with the results. In the stillness of the night, she wept in surrender to God. Tomorrow, after church, she would pull Michael aside and tell him the truth about her upbringing. He would either understand or he wouldn't, but at least she would no longer be living a lie.

thirteen

An icy wind whipped around Michael, and he urged his horse to a trot. He pulled his collar higher and tucked in his chin to protect himself from the blast. The ride from Oregon City didn't take as long on horseback as it did in a wagon laden with supplies, but it was still a good three-hour ride, and he hoped to be home before the snow got too deep. But before he could head back to the farm, he had to do what he came to do.

Ma had balked at his intention to travel to Oregon City on the Lord's Day, but Michael couldn't wait to settle things with Star's guardian. He didn't know for sure whom he was even looking for, but decided to keep an eye out for Clem. The man was pretty unique in appearance and might be easily identified if he asked around. So far, Michael had been riding through the streets and no one he asked knew the man—or if they did, they weren't forthcoming with the information.

There are things you don't know about me. Things that would change how you feel. After Star's tearful words last night, he'd decided to pay the man the money she took so she could be out from under the burden of guilt. When he returned home, he intended to ask her to be his wife.

The streets were nearly empty, so there weren't many people to talk to. Finally, he saw a couple of men staggering out of a saloon at the edge of town. Deciding to give his search one last try, he approached the men.

"Excuse me!" he called. They stopped and waited while he dismounted and tethered his horse to the hitching post.

"Whaddaya want, Mister?" one of the men asked, slurring his words.

Michael stepped onto the boardwalk. "I'm looking for a

man named Clem. Big fella with a black moustache and a scar running down his cheek. Ever seen him?"

"Maybe. What's it worth to you?"

Disgusted, Michael fished a couple of coins out of his pocket and handed them over. "Now, do you know Clem or not?"

"Yeah, works for Luke."

"Where can I find him?"

The man who'd taken the money jerked his thumb toward the saloon. "At Luke's. Where else?"

Michael's stomach tightened as he lifted his head and read the sign. *Luke's Saloon.* Star's guardian owned a saloon? Without another look at the two drunks who'd sold him the information he was no longer sure he even wanted, he walked to the saloon. It went against everything inside of him to step through those swinging doors. A few men glanced up from a card game in the corner of the room, then ignored him. Cautiously, he stepped up to the counter.

"What can I get for you, Mister?" the bartender asked. His burly chest stuck out; and even at Michael's height, he was forced to lift his chin in order to meet the man's gaze.

"I'm looking for a man named Luke. I think he owns this place."

"What do you want with him?"

"That's my business."

The man's arm shot out, and he grabbed a fistful of Michael's shirt before he could evade the attack. "I'm making it my business. No one bothers Luke without a good reason."

Michael swallowed hard. He couldn't very well get into a barroom brawl. Better that he just tell the man what he wanted to know. "Turn me loose, and I'll tell you."

The man let go, giving him a little shove in the process. Michael caught his footing in time to keep from crashing to the ground. He adjusted his shirt and cleared his throat. "I want to discuss a mutual acquaintance with him."

"Who's that?"

Releasing a heavy sigh, Michael leaned in. "A young woman named Star."

"Star, you say?" The bartender narrowed his gaze and studied Michael's face.

"Yes. Can you keep your voice down?"

"Stay where you are," the man commanded. "Luke's going to want to talk to you."

A minute later he returned, accompanied by a painted woman wearing a satin gown, cut high to reveal her thigh and low at the top, leaving little to the imagination. "Follow me," she purred.

Michael's face burned as she led him up the stairs. He kept his gaze fixed on the steps and nearly stumbled when they reached the top. The saloon girl wrapped her fingers around his upper arm. "Careful, Cowboy. Wouldn't want you to break your handsome neck." As though he'd been burned, Michael jerked away. "I'm fine," he said abruptly. "Just take me to Luke."

"Well, ain't you just the charmer?" She let out a laugh and reached out to trace his jaw with a long, red fingernail.

"Please, Lady, just leave me alone."

"Star's got you all spoken for, eh?"

"Something like that."

Thankfully, he wasn't forced to carry on any more conversation as she opened a large, ornately carved door at the end of the hall. "Here he is, Luke." She winked broadly at him and blew him a kiss.

Michael scowled and crossed the threshold. A handsome man with graying temples stood behind a large desk. He met Michael in the center of the room and extended his hand. "I understand you have some information about one of my girls."

Taking the proffered hand, Michael frowned at the reference to Star as one of Luke's "girls."

"Star Campbell. I'm here to pay off her debt to you."

The man took a cigar and silently offered one to Michael. Michael waved his refusal. "Have a seat, Mr. . . ?"

"Riley. Michael Riley." Michael accepted the wing chair across from Luke. "About Star?"

"Ahh, yes. Star. How touching she should consider me her guardian." A puff of smoke found its way to Michael's senses, nearly choking him.

"What do you mean? Clem told me you're her guardian."

Luke narrowed his gaze. "Clem?" A look of understanding crossed his dark features. "You must be the man Clem ran into the day Star disappeared." His voice was colder than the snow outside, but Michael refused to be intimidated.

"That's right. I intend to marry her, but first I want to settle what she owes you."

Luke released a hoarse laugh that never quite reached his eyes. "As much as I'd love to divest you of your money, Mr. Riley, I'm afraid Star doesn't owe me a cent."

"What do you mean?"

"What I mean is that I'm not Star's guardian. I'm her boss. In other words, she works for me. Here."

"But then why was Clem. . . ?"

"Running after her?"

"Yes."

Waving away the question, Luke took another puff of his cigar. "To tell you the truth, Star and I had a misunderstanding, and she ran out before I could explain. I sent Clem to bring her back. Your intervention thwarted his efforts, and I haven't seen Star since. I miss her, and so do the men who come in here."

Michael's heart plummeted at the inference. "What do you mean?" he asked, his voice barely audible.

Giving a nod of understanding, Luke sighed. "I suppose I can't blame Star for not wanting to admit to her—er—profession. It looks to me as though she's duped you and probably your entire town. Am I right?"

Numb with disappointment, Michael gave a nearly imperceptible nod.

"Well, if you decide not to marry her, she is welcome back here anytime. The men still ask for her quite frequently. She was a favorite around here. I'm sure I don't have to tell you why that would be." His suggestive leer sickened Michael, and he shot to his feet, knowing if he didn't leave this minute, he'd smash his fist into the suave face.

"I'm sorry I bothered you," he said abruptly. "I'll let myself out."

"Remember what I said now. Tell Star we miss her."

There are things you don't know about me. Things that would change how you feel.

Star's words took on new meaning. Feeling like an utter fool, Michael walked through the saloon in a haze. He mounted his horse and headed out of town at a full gallop. Now everything made sense. The way she'd defended the saloon girl the night before. What an utter fool he'd been! How had he fallen in love with another loose woman? He laughed at himself. The kiss must have been carefully executed on her part for her to make him believe she'd never been kissed before. Hysterical laughter rose to his throat. Never been kissed! The woman he loved—a prostitute. Laughter gave way to tears and suddenly he pulled his horse to a halt and slid from the saddle and to his knees.

"God!" he shouted at the snow-laden clouds. "Where are You in all of this? Am I a fool? Did I misunderstand when I believed I was to help Star?" He hung his head and cried until the tears would come no longer. Snow soaked into the bottom half of his trousers as he stayed on his knees. When he finally climbed to his feet, he mounted his horse with a new determination. First thing in the morning, he would confront Star, then he'd inform the folks who thought they could trust her that there was a wolf in their midst.

She'd regret playing him for a fool.

❧

Monday mornings always depressed Star. After the glory of

worship services on Sunday and the restful afternoons spent visiting with Rosemary and Mrs. Barker, the thought of returning to the mundane always left her feeling a bit let down. If Joe had his way, she would work on Sundays; but at the risk of losing the job, she'd absolutely put her foot down from the first day of her employment. To her relief, he'd given in without much of a fight.

Today, her heart sank even farther into depression as Joe let her into the restaurant at eight o'clock to start baking biscuits to last the day. Michael had been absent from church yesterday. After Miss Hannah had assured her that he wasn't ill, she remained tight-lipped about where he had gone.

Star was in no mood for Jane's stinging insults nor Joe's grouchy commands. Only a day and a half had passed since she'd seen Michael, and already it seemed as if a decade had gone by. With a sigh, she hung her coat on a hook and grabbed an apron.

She began pulling ingredients down from the shelf, then glanced about with a frown. "Is Jane ill today?"

Joe mumbled and pulled out his handkerchief. He blew his nose loudly and stuffed it back. "She's packin' her things."

"What do you mean?" For the first time, Star realized Joe's eyes were moist and his nose red. The man had enough heart to cry? "Joe, what's wrong?"

Fresh tears assaulted him. "My girl's leavin' me."

"Why on earth is she doing that?"

He scowled. "I told her to get out. That's why."

Mouth agape, Star blinked. "That doesn't make sense. Why would you send her away and then cry about it? What's happened?"

"I'm with child." The inflectionless response came from the kitchen door.

Joe stiffened and turned away.

"Are you sure?"

The girl straightened her shoulders and nodded, her expression haughty.

"Where's the baby's father? Does he know about this?"

A short, mirthless laugh left Jane's lips. "I don't know for sure who the father is." She glanced at Joe, almost as though the words were meant as poisoned arrows.

The arrows hit their mark, and Joe slammed a ladle against the stove. He swung about to face his daughter. "How could you shame me this way? How could you shame the memory of your mother?"

"Oh, Pa." Jane sighed and dropped to a stool. "I'm leaving so you aren't shamed in this town."

"You've shamed me already." Anger burned in his eyes.

Star knelt before Jane and took her hands. "Is there anything I can do to help?"

"I don't see what you can do. I got myself into this fix. There's nothing to do but go away and have the baby and find a good home for it."

"My sweet Ella's only grandbaby given away to be raised by strangers." Joe's muttered words of pain brought hope to Star.

"Joe, it seems as though you might be willing to help Jane raise this baby. Are you sure you want her to go away?"

"Don't waste your breath, Star," Jane said. "Once my pa makes up his mind, he doesn't relent."

"Of course he does. He hired me back, didn't he?"

Jane gave her a withering glance. "That's hardly the same thing."

"You're right, it isn't. I'm not his daughter. You are, and he loves you more than anything in this world." *God, please give me the right words.*

Joe cleared his throat. "I guess you could stay on, if you want."

Jane's eyes filled with tears. "Thank you, Pa. I know how hard it is for you to even consider being the talk of the town. But what good will it do to stay here? The whole town will be against me and my baby. My child will grow up hating me for ruining his or her life. It's better if I go away and come back alone."

Tell her, Daughter.

Star blinked at the words she heard impressed upon her heart. Not so much in words, but a gentle understanding, a knowing what God was asking her to do. She gathered a breath. How could she admit where she'd come from? Her hands trembled as she gently pressed Jane's hands.

"My mother raised me alone," she began.

The look of utter disdain she received from Jane nearly broke her resolve. "Raising a child alone because your husband is gone is not the same thing as raising a child alone because you got in a fix and don't even know who the baby's father is." She jerked her hand away from Star's and stood abruptly. Gathering her bag, she glanced at Joe. "I guess I best be going. I'll wait at the stage office until the stagecoach arrives."

"That won't be for hours," Joe said. "Why not stay here until it gets into town?"

"It'll just be harder to go, Pa. Good-bye."

Star watched her leave through the kitchen door.

Don't let her leave without telling her.

Following her into the dining room, Star called out to her. "Wait, Jane."

A longsuffering sigh left the girl, but she stopped and turned around. "What is it, Star? More bleeding heart acceptance? I appreciate that you haven't seemed the judgmental sort. If it means anything to you, you're the only woman I've ever felt friendly toward. But I don't need your stories. I don't need you to preach to me. I just need you to let me go." Her lip quivered, and before Star's eyes, the unimaginable happened: Some of Jane's bravado crumbled.

Encouraged, Star slipped her arm about Jane's shoulders. She held her with a firm grip and led her to the dining area and a table. "Please sit down. I would like to tell you something. You have plenty of time."

"All right. But only because if I don't, you'll follow me to the station."

Star grinned. "You're right. I probably would."

"I'm listening."

"As I said, my mother raised me alone. And it *wasn't* because my father died." She hesitated as Jane's brow arched. "The truth is that my mother was a saloon girl. I don't even know who my father was."

A look of disbelief crossed Jane's face.

"It's true. I was raised over one saloon or another until a few months ago when my mother was murdered." The familiar anger burned inside her at the memory. She pushed it aside for now. "The man who owned the saloon tried to make me take her place, but I ran away before he could force me to sell myself."

"But what about all this talk about God? You're no better than I am. Even if you never actually sold yourself to men, you're still the daughter of a prostitute. At least my ma was a respectable church-going woman."

Clearly, in Jane's mind, that fact raised herself to a place just above Star. "That's just it, Jane. I know I'm no better than you are. Or anyone. Jesus sees us for who we are on the inside."

"You were really raised in a saloon? How could your mother do that?"

Star bristled a bit at the criticism of her mother, but she swallowed her quick anger, knowing God had a purpose for her conversation with Jane. "My ma never left her life because she didn't believe she could do any better. She had no one to go to, and she had me to raise."

"You didn't hate her?"

"Never!" Star replied emphatically. "I loved her more than anything in the whole world. And your child will love you too. Children are that way."

"How can I do that to a child? Do you know how people will treat my baby?"

Star nodded. "It's possible some folks will be cruel, but you're strong, Jane. You'll have your pa to help you too. Most women in your situation aren't so blessed."

"Listen to the girl, Jane." Star turned to find Joe standing in the kitchen doorway. He walked toward the table. "I won't let anyone say a word against my daughter or my grandchild. If they do, I'll refuse them service in my restaurant." He sat in the chair next to her and took her hands in his gnarled ones. "I don't want you to go. I've not done right by you. Haven't been a good pa. Your ma would be heartbroken if she knew how I've acted. But if you'll give me another chance, I'll do better with my grandchild."

Feeling like an intruder, Star was about to excuse herself when a knock sounded at the door. Joe gave a huff. "When are folks gonna get it through their heads that I don't open one minute before eleven o'clock?"

Star stood and placed a hand on his shoulder. "I'll see who it is." She glanced closer through the glass window, and her heart thudded in her chest. "May I have the key to open the door, Joe? It's Michael."

"All right. This time. But tell him he can't have anything to eat this early."

Star walked toward the door. She noticed that Michael's face held far from an amiable expression. His eyes blazed. She unlocked and opened the door. He stomped inside and grabbed her arm. None too gently.

"What is it, Michael? What's happened?"

A sneer twisted his lips. "What's happened? I'll tell you. I went to see Luke."

Star felt the blood drain from her cheeks. Pressing her palm flat against her stomach, she stared mutely at him.

"Didn't expect that, did you?"

Feeling dizzy, Star dropped into the nearest chair. "D—did you tell him where to find me?"

Michael placed his hands flat on the table and bent at the waist. His stormy gaze commanded hers, and Star cringed at the look of disdain. "That's it? That's all you care about? Whether or not I told him where you're at? It doesn't matter to you that I know about you?"

"I—I was going to tell you, Michael. Honestly, I planned to tell you all about Luke and the saloon yesterday, but you weren't at church. I guess now I know why."

"That's a very convenient story."

"Everything okay, Star?" Joe asked from the other end of the room.

"Y—yes. Everything's fine."

"Michael, I'm sorry my past upsets you so. I know I should have been honest from the very beginning. I just didn't have the courage."

"It's good for you that you weren't honest in the beginning, or I'd have never exposed my daughter to you. I was tempted to ruin your name, but I've changed my mind. This is between you and me. But stay away from my family or, so help me, I might change my mind again."

His boots resonated on the wooden floor as he made his way to the door.

Finding her courage, Star hurried after him. "You can be angry with me all you want, Michael, but I know I'm a child of God. Who I was before is wiped away. I'm just sorry you're so set in your ways that you can't see that."

She slammed the door behind him without giving him a chance to answer. He stood on the boardwalk, staring at her through the window while she locked the door. With a final look at him, she turned and walked to the kitchen.

Jane stood at the counter, mixing up dough for biscuits. She shook her head sadly. "You see?" she said, her voice filled with resignation. "That's what my baby has to look forward to."

Fighting back her tears, Star nodded. "Some people will turn you away, Jane. But God never will. Won't you consider giving Him a chance?"

Jane hesitated. "I'll think about it, Star. I give you my word that I will."

That was all she could ask and more than she'd hoped for.

They worked hard to open the doors at eleven, and Star barely had a chance to breathe all day. Snow fell steadily by the time she walked outside that night after twelve hours of work. She headed toward the street, trying to keep her boots from sliding on the icy surface. Just as she stepped off the boardwalk, she felt a hand on her arm. Her heart leapt.

"Michael. . . ," she breathed.

"Not quite," a familiar mocking voice said against her ear as a man clamped his hand over her mouth. "Now you be a good girl and don't scream and maybe I'll let you live until Luke decides what to do with you."

Tears filled Star's eyes as Clem led her toward two horses waiting across the street in front of the saloon.

Jesus, if You will, please help me.

fourteen

After two hours of staring at the ceiling, Michael finally gave up his quest for sleep. He swung his legs around and sat upright on his bed. Resting his elbows on his knees, he sought answers from God.

How could You allow me to fall in love with another prostitute? How? You knew I wanted to find a virtuous, godly woman to share my life with and to help raise my daughter. It was bad enough that I fell in love with Star when I thought she was just a thief—but a saloon girl?

The snow had finally come to an end outside and the moon had risen. Now it streamed through his window and illuminated his Bible, sitting unopened on his nightstand. He picked up the Bible and let it fall open. He wanted to read something to assure him he was right, that he hadn't been unreasonable—as Ma had said outright when he'd returned home and divulged the information he'd received in Oregon City.

She'd quoted him every Scripture about God throwing sins into the sea and all the ones about His mercy and grace. Michael didn't want to hear it. If Star had truly repented, why hadn't she just told them the truth? Omission was the same as lying, so she'd been lying from the moment he'd found her asleep in the hay.

In an effort to push the memory of her lovely, sleeping face aside, he lit the lamp, stretched back out on the bed, propped against his pillows, and let his gaze fall to the Bible.

"He raiseth up the poor out of the dust, and lifteth the needy out of the dunghill; that he may set him with princes, even with the princes of his people. He maketh the barren woman, a joyful mother of children. Praise ye the Lord."

Star's words came rushing back to him.

Not one little girl is born with a desire to grow up and become a prostitute. We all dream of marrying our handsome prince and raising babies, taking care of a home.

Was God trying to tell him something by using the words "prince" and "joyful mother of children"? Not that Michael was a prince by any means, but Star loved him. Or she seemed to. Ma certainly felt she loved him and Aimee. He'd called women like Star "trash." Was God telling him He had raised her out of the dunghill and sent her to him so he could be her prince and make her a mother to his child?

Kneeling beside his bed, Michael cried out to God. "I love her. You know I do. What do I do with the thoughts of her being with other men?"

My love is perfect and unconditional. Let Me love her through you. Trust Me.

Time stood still as Michael surrendered his bitterness and disappointment to God. When, at last, his tears were spent, he knew he had to go and see Star. He would beg her forgiveness, and if she'd have him, he'd marry her on the spot.

A loud knock at the door interrupted his planning, and with a frown, he pulled on his trousers, grabbed the lamp, and headed down the ladder.

He opened the door.

"Oh, good—I have the right farm. It took me all night to find you."

"Miss Grafton?" Michael opened the door wider and allowed Jane entrance. "What on earth are you doing?"

"Mr. Riley, it's about Star."

Michael's heart jumped. "What about her?"

"I saw a man speaking to her after she left the restaurant tonight. At first I thought you had returned, but I realized when he seemed to be holding her against her will that it wasn't you. He took her across to the saloon and made her get on a horse, then they both rode out of town."

Grabbing Jane by the arms, he shook her. "What did the man look like? Was there a scar on his face?"

"P–please, Mr. Riley. I don't know. The street was dark. It was still snowing."

Michael turned her loose and raked his hands through his hair. If anything happened to Star, it would be all his fault. He'd led Clem right to her.

❧

Shivering and weary, Star nonetheless refused to cower before Luke's frighteningly controlled anger. "So our little Star has returned. Shame on you for worrying me so much all these months."

He stood directly in front of her, towering over her. She flinched as he reached forward and traced his finger down her cheek. "Silly girl, there's no need to worry. I wouldn't bruise this beautiful face." His gaze traveled over her frame, and Star stiffened. He made her feel undressed. When he looked at her again, she couldn't keep the defiance from her eyes.

"You don't want to rebel, Star," he said, his voice calm, but filled with warning. "You remember what happened to your mother?"

Anger raged inside of Star. She'd bottled it for so long, in an effort to forgive Luke, that it came back in such a rush, it surprised her and loosened her tongue before she could stop herself. "You murdering thug. If you think you're going to get away with killing my mother, you're sadly mistaken."

"Is that so?"

"I'll go to the sheriff and tell him what I saw."

"The sheriff knows all about your mother's unfortunate demise at the hands of one of her rougher customers. A drifter. A man long gone before we even found her poor, broken body."

Fury engulfed her, and she flew at Luke, beating him with her fists. He held her off easily. "Calm down before I'm forced to tie your hands."

Chest heaving from the effort, Star glared at him. "You make me sick," she hissed.

His brow rose, and he narrowed his gaze; but true to character, Luke remained calm, as he did whenever it suited his purposes. "Now, I know you're acting this way because you're so tired. So rather than punish you for your hurtful comments, I intend to let you readjust to the saloon. You can have your old room back. But be warned: My patience won't last forever. Don't try to run away. Clem will be just outside your door. I'll give you today to rest, but tomorrow you will begin working. Oh, don't look so horrified. It won't be so bad once you get used to it. Just ask the other girls."

He cupped her cheeks and pressed a hard kiss to her forehead. "It's wonderful to see you again, my dear."

Star's stomach revolted at the feel of his wet kiss. She shuddered and stepped back.

His eyes narrowed. "Be a good girl, and you'll be rewarded. Be stubborn, and you'll suffer the consequences. Be impossible, and you'll be dead."

"I'd rather be dead than do what you're suggesting."

"We'll see." Going to the door, he motioned for Clem. "Escort Star to her room. And fetch Lila to bring her a tray."

"Lila? She isn't dead?"

"Of course not. Where would you get such an idea?"

Star scowled at Clem. "Where indeed? Last I saw her, she was on the floor, and Clem was about to beat her down."

"She's fine."

"What about Samson?"

Luke hesitated. "I'm afraid he couldn't be saved."

Tears stung Star's eyes. At least Lila was alive. She wasn't completely alone.

With his heart pounding in his ears, Michael rode his horse much faster than he should have over the snowy ground. When he stopped in front of Luke's Saloon, he barely took the time to tether the horse to the hitching post before bursting through the door.

The same bartender as before stood behind the counter. Michael didn't bother to stop this time. Instead, he headed straight for the stairs and took them three at a time.

"Hey, what do you think you're doing?"

Michael heard the gruff voice calling behind him, but he kept his focus on the door at the end of the hall. During the ride, he'd made plans in his mind, and he'd known he would have to take them by surprise and not stop to ask permission. He burst into Luke's office. A woman gasped and shot from the saloon owner's lap. She hurried past Michael and scurried out the open door.

A flicker of alarm passed over Luke's face, but he recovered so quickly it was as though he had been expecting Michael in the first place. He grabbed a cigar from his case on the desk, bit off the end, and lit the disgusting stick.

"We meet again, Mr. . .Riley, was it?"

Rough hands seized him from behind. "Sorry about that, Luke, he ran past before I could stop him."

Waving his bouncer away, Luke kept his gaze focused on Michael. "It's all right, Jack. Mr. Riley is my guest. For now, anyway. Go back to the bar and close the door on your way out."

Reluctantly, the burly bartender turned him loose. Michael could tell he'd have preferred the opportunity to give him a good pounding. He'd most likely get the chance to try before all was said and done, but Michael knew God was on his side. Somehow, he'd get to Star and take her out of this evil place.

When they were alone, Luke motioned toward the same

chair Michael had occupied during their last visit. "Now, tell me why you're here."

"You know exactly what I came for."

"Star?" He gave a short laugh. "I'm afraid she's a bit tired from the trip. I gave her the night off. One of our other ladies perhaps?"

Fury burned inside of Michael at the man's crude inference. "Star isn't going back to that life. We both know she was forced. I've come to take her home."

"That's where we differ, Mr. Riley." Luke leaned forward, his eyes no longer hinting at friendliness. "I say she's staying here where she belongs."

"Star belongs with me, and I intend to marry her." Wheeling about, he strode to the door. "Star!" he called as he stepped out of the room. "Where are you?"

He noticed Clem standing in front of a door at the other end of the hall. The man was poised to fight. Michael closed the distance between them in a few long strides. "She's in there?"

"You're not getting past me."

"Michael, is that you?" Star's voice came through the closed door.

"It's me, Honey. I'm here to take you home."

"Oh, thank you, Lord."

"I don't think so, Bub."

Michael turned just as a fist connected with his face. Everything went out of focus for an instant. Blinking, he tried to stop the spinning. The bartender took the opportunity and grabbed him by the collar. He practically carried him down the steps and tossed him out the door. Michael took a second to gather his wits, then he barreled back through the door. He made a run for the steps again, but this time the bartender had help. Four men stopped him, but instead of throwing him out the front, they carried him toward the kitchen.

"Star! I'll find a way, I promise. I love you! I'll be back!" he called.

"You don't learn so good." Those were the only words he heard before everything went black.

Everything hurt when he woke up, freezing and lying in the alley behind the saloon. His first conscious thought was that they must have mistaken him for dead—either that or they'd left him to die. He shivered and winced as pain shot through his middle. Gritting his teeth determinedly against the pain, he forced himself to his feet. He knew if he returned to the saloon they'd kill him, but better to die trying to save the woman he loved than to walk away and seal her fate.

One eye was swollen completely shut and his mouth felt puffy. He knew he had broken ribs. He also knew he had to go back inside. He stumbled to the kitchen door and opened it a crack. Through his one good eye, he perused the room. A black woman stood peeling potatoes at a table in the center of the kitchen.

Cautiously, he opened the door wide enough to gain entrance.

The woman glanced up, her eyes went wide, and she drew back in horror, confirming to Michael that he looked about as bad as he felt.

"Star." He managed to say through his swollen lips. "I. . . need. . .to. . .get. . .to. . .her. I. . .won't. . .hurt. . .you."

She chuckled. "I ain't fearin' that one bit. You cain't hurt nothin' like that. My girl say you be comin' back. I tole her you was probly dead."

"Not yet."

A tender smile touched the slave woman's face. "You be wantin' ter marry my Star?"

He nodded.

"Well, you wind up dead if you goes through there." She jerked her thumb toward the door leading to the main room.

"Come on, Lila show you which room. Don' know how you plan ter get her out, though."

"Let. . .me. . .worry. . .about. . .that."

She gave him a doubtful look, but took him back outside to the alleyway. They walked a few steps, then she stopped and pointed at a lighted window. "Dat be my Star's room."

"Thank you." He bent and kissed the dark, withered cheek. "Get back inside before you're missed."

He glanced around. How could he climb up there in his condition?

"Hey, Cowboy!"

With a groan, Michael glanced back toward the kitchen door. The same woman who'd escorted him up the stairs during his last visit to Luke's stood, her face a mask of amusement.

"Do you really think you can climb up there in your condition?"

"I have to try."

"You'll get yourself killed."

A shrug lifted his shoulders. "She's worth it."

"Is she? Well, then lucky for you, Lila told me she brought you out here. That little old woman stayed here, sure Luke would bring Star back somehow. She wasn't about to leave Star alone with him."

"So why did she get you?"

"Lila knows I can help."

Michael looked at her, defenses alerted. "Why would you do that?"

"Well, for one thing, Star's mother was my friend. I've known Star since she was a little girl. If she has a chance at a better life, I owe it to her mother to do everything I can to help."

Michael nodded. "All right. Then how do I get up there?"

"You don't. You'll kill yourself."

"I thought you said you wanted to help."

"If you'll trust me, I can help you. My way. Is that your hat on the ground?"

He looked to where she pointed. "Yes."

"Grab it and come on. By the way, my name's Tina."

"Michael."

Still not sure what Tina was up to, Michael nevertheless knew he had no choice but to trust her. Once he was back in the kitchen, she reached up and adjusted his hat so that it nearly covered his face. "All right, Michael. Put your arm around me."

Michael drew back in alarm.

She scowled. "You're going to have to pretend you like me, Cowboy. That's the only way to get you upstairs. Once we're there, don't go half-cocked and take off after Clem like you did before. It was brave, but incredibly stupid."

"What do you have in mind?"

"First, I'm going to take you into my room like you're a customer." She gave him a wry grin. "Still with me?"

He scowled as well as he could through his swollen face. "Yeah."

"I'll call for Clem, and when he comes in, I'll whack him over the head with a lamp. Then you can sneak into Star's room."

"What about the lock?"

"Luke doesn't believe in locks. That's why Clem was standing guard."

"All right. Let's go."

Michael trembled as he put his arm around the strongly perfumed woman. She laughed uproariously as though he'd said the funniest thing as they made their way through the kitchen door and toward the staircase. Michael prayed fervently that no one recognized his clothes. He'd tucked his shirt back in and brushed off his trousers to appear a bit more presentable. Playing his role, he nuzzled Tina's neck, eliciting another round of giggles from her. They nuzzled and giggled all the way up the steps. Each step burned like fire, and he nearly fainted from the pain. Michael stumbled when they reached the landing.

"Easy, Cowboy," Tina said. "You've had a little too much whiskey tonight."

"You all right, Tina?"

Michael stiffened at the sound of Clem's voice, but Tina laughed and waved the thug off. "I'm fine. This cowboy's had a bit too much to drink, but I can handle him. I'll call if I need you."

She led him to a room. "All right," she said when the door was safely shut behind them. "Take a minute to catch your breath. You okay?"

Every inch of his body hurt, but Michael knew this was his one shot to rescue Star. He nodded. "I'll be fine."

"You're a real hero," she said pensively. She turned her back to him. "Unbutton me."

Michael frowned and drew back. "I don't know what you thought, but—"

"Just do it," she snapped. "When you leave, take my dress for Star to put on. Our hair is close to the same color. If you leave down the steps with her, she can keep her face turned so the bartender doesn't see her. The room's so crowded, no one will look close enough to make sure the girl in the red dress is the same one you went upstairs with." She tossed him the gown. "When you get to the main room downstairs, keep going and leave by the front door. The girls walk their customers out all the time. No one will think anything of it. Once you get outside, don't stop, and you should be safe."

"What about you? Won't you get into trouble?"

Again she waved her hand. "Clem won't know what hit him. I'm good at talking my way out of trouble."

"Thank you," he said, pressing her hands.

Her eyes misted and she quickly looked away. Grabbing a glass lamp from a nearby table, she screamed, "Clem!"

Seconds later, he burst through the door. "Tina, what's—"
Crash!

The lamp found its mark, and Clem fell unconscious to the ground.

Tina looked into the hallway. "Hurry!"

With the red satin gown slung over his arm, Michael rushed to Star's room. He flung open the door and shut it quickly after him.

"Michael!" She flew into his arms, knocking the breath from him. "Oh, my love. I thought they'd killed you." As much as he relished having her in his arms, he pushed her gently from him.

Her lips quivered. "Michael, I'm so sorry I wasn't honest with you from the very first day."

"It's all right. We have a lot to talk about, Honey, but for now put this on."

Star gasped as she glanced at the gown.

"Trust me," he urged.

Hesitantly she took the dress. Michael faced the door. Listening to the rustle of the satin behind him, he inwardly cringed, hating the thought that she'd have to wear the immodest garment.

"I–I'm ready," she said a moment later, her voice trembling and barely above a whisper.

Michael gathered a sharp breath at the sight of her. The pain in his stomach extended from the physical to a very emotional pain.

She lowered her gaze, her face ashen. "I love you," she whispered. "I'm sorry to bring you into such a mess."

He went to her and drew her gently into his arms. "I love you too. You'll never have need to be ashamed again, my love."

Pulling away, he cupped her cheeks and gently kissed her lips, despite the pain in his own.

"How touching."

Looking past Michael, Star gasped. "Luke!"

Nausea seized Star at the sight of Luke standing in the doorway, holding a gun on them. His face held no hint of its usual calm. Instead, the veins in his neck bulged. He sneered. "You look lovely, Star. Finally dressed as you should be." Turning his attention to Michael, Luke gave a mocking grin. "It appears as though you can't be taught a lesson, Mr. Riley. I believe I made it clear that Star remains with me."

Michael pulled Star into the circle of his arm. "And I told you, I'm taking her home."

"Ah, yes. You intend to make her the little wife. But don't you realize what having babies will do to her figure?"

Heat burned Star's cheeks even as she realized that he'd said Michael intended to make her his wife. Joy bubbled inside of her, pushing back the fear.

"What do you intend to do?" Michael asked.

"Well, unfortunately for me, the sheriff came in to get himself a beer. If I shoot you right now, he'll hear it, and I doubt I could make him believe another drifter killed you. It looks like we'll have to wait here until the sheriff finishes his drink."

He stepped forward. "Now, turn loose of my girl, please."

"She's not your girl," Michael said through gritted teeth.

"She'll be dead if you don't do as I said."

Unwilling to take a chance that Luke might fly into a rage and harm Michael, Star stepped away from the warmth of his arm.

Luke rewarded her with a smile. "That's a good girl. If you keep being cooperative, I won't have to punish you too much."

"You won't touch her," Michael said.

"Is that so?" Luke's free hand shot out and grabbed Star. She gasped as his fingers bit painfully into her bare arm. "Let's get one thing straight before you die. I will touch her anytime I choose and however I choose." Keeping his gun pointed at Michael's chest, he brought his mouth down hard on Star's. She fought against him; and in that wretched moment when his cold lips punished hers, she brought her hands flat against his chest and shoved as hard as she could. Then before he could get his bearings, she grabbed his hand that held the gun and knocked the weapon onto the floor. Racing forward, Star kicked it toward Michael.

"Why you. . ." Cold hatred shot from Luke's eyes. "You'll regret that." He brought his hand up.

"I wouldn't advise that." Michael's tone carried a deadly threat. Star held her breath as Luke's arm remained poised to strike. With a sneer, he gave in and dropped his arm to his side. Michael motioned him to a straight-backed wooden chair. "Get something to tie him up with, Star."

Glancing about, Star felt as helpless as a kitten until she spotted a corset hanging from a peg in the corner. She grabbed the garment and pulled out the strings. "This is all I could find."

Michael scowled. "That won't hold him for long, but it'll give us time to get out of here. Take the gun and keep it aimed at him."

Star took the weapon. Luke's lips twisted into a smirk. "Do you really think I'm going to let you go? All this is, is a little setback. Even if you do get out of here, we know where to find you. Make no mistake, Star. I'll come after you."

"Shut up, Luke," Michael said as he wound the corset strings around the meaty wrists.

Ignoring Michael's threatening tone, Luke continued to bait. "I recognized you'd be a great beauty even when you were a little girl. Why do you think I kept your mother around as long as I did? I should have kicked her out five years ago, and I would have if not for you. She barely earned enough to feed and clothe the two of you, but I knew once you were old enough, you'd more than make up for what she cost me."

Fury began to build inside of Star. *Oh, God, help me.* Her finger rested on the trigger. She'd never fired a gun before, but at this range, she knew she couldn't miss.

"Shut up, Luke," she whispered. "Just stop talking."

"Come now, Star. What are you going to do? Kill me? After I raised you as though you were my own daughter? You're as ungrateful as your filthy mother was. After all I did for her, she had the nerve to threaten to take you and leave. I had to kill her, and I'd do it again."

Star's world zeroed in on one thing. . .the fact that she held the means to avenge her mother's death. All it would take was a little more pressure and Luke would be dead.

"Give me the gun, Star." Star barely heard Michael's voice through the fog of memories that roared through her mind. She heard her mother's scream. Heard Luke's taunting confession. *Lord, he deserves to die.* Tears flooded her eyes as her mind filled with the image of Jesus on the cross. She couldn't do it. No matter how much she believed he deserved to die, Jesus had died for him too, and she had no right to take his life. She handed the gun to Michael. "Take it," she said hoarsely.

The door burst open at that moment. Tina, accompanied by the sheriff, walked into the room.

"It's a good thing you're here, Sheriff," Luke said. "These two were about to rob me. I want them arrested."

"Save it. We heard every word you said to the girl. You just talked yourself into a murder charge, Luke."

Protesting all the way, Luke was escorted out by the sheriff. Star smiled at Tina. "I don't know how we can thank you for all you've done."

The woman's face grew red. "Think nothing of it. I guess now we all gotta start thinking about another place to work." She winked at the two of them. "Unless I can find me a cowboy like yours." With a grin, she left them.

Star caught her breath and sat hard on the bed. "Oh, Michael. I almost killed him." She covered her face with her hands.

He came to her and knelt before her. "Shh," he said, taking her hands from her face and holding them firmly. "The important thing is, you didn't."

"I'm just so glad it's over, and Luke won't be able to hurt anyone else."

Michael nodded. "So am I." He captured her gaze. "I'm glad all of this is behind us and we can get on with our life together."

He stroked her hand with his thumb.

"Our life together?" she whispered, afraid to believe it.

Pressing her hands to his lips, he kissed each knuckle, then looked up to capture her gaze. "I was so wrong. I accused you of not being a decent woman, when the truth is that anything in the past is gone.

"When Luke told me what you were, I went crazy with jealousy that other men had touched you."

"Michael. . ."

"Let me finish." He kissed her hand again. "I sought the Lord long and hard about this, and I know that I have no right to hold something against you that He forgot the moment you confessed it. I don't have to be ashamed or afraid to love you and make you my wife. You're as pure as the day you were born as far as God is concerned. And as far as I'm concerned as well."

Tears flowed down Star's cheeks. Pulling her hands gently from his, she slid from the bed to the floor and knelt beside him. "Oh, Michael. Luke told you I was one of his girls?"

"Yes, my love. But it doesn't matter. I want you to be my wife and Aimee's mother." His brown eyes filled with tears. "I never want to be without you again. Tell me you'll marry me."

"Of course, I will. But, Michael, you have to know something."

"What's that?

Placing her palm against his cheek, she smiled. "Darling, I am coming to you pure."

"I know, Honey. I know."

"No, you don't know." He was being so noble, she almost didn't have the heart to tell him. "Luke lied to you. I was never one of his girls. That's why I ran away in the first place—because he was going to force me to work for him. When I say I'm coming to you untouched, I mean it."

Joy lit his eyes, and he gathered her to him. Star pulled away, and for the next few minutes, she told him her story. Of Luke murdering her mother, of Lila and Sam loving her all of her life and helping her get away from Luke, of her fear that if she told him where she'd come from he might turn her out.

Michael gathered her close once more. "I might have," he admitted. "But God's changed me. I only want to make you happy."

The door flew open, and Lila's tiny frame made an imposing figure in the doorway. Her stormy gaze rested on Michael. "Turn her loose. It ain't proper, you holdin' on to Star when you's alone like dis."

Michael inclined his head. "You're right, Ma'am. And since it appears you are the closest thing Star has to family, I suppose I'll be asking your permission for her hand in marriage."

Lila's face lit up like a Roman candle. "In dat case, I guess I'm gonna have ter say yes."

A lopsided grin split Michael's face. He squeezed Star's hand, then glanced back up to Lila. "Will you come and live with us?"

Quick tears misted Lila's black eyes. "You knows I will."

"Oh, Michael," Star whispered. "What a wonderful idea!"

"Yes. Ma'll be relieved. She still needs that help." He gave Star a teasing grin.

Star's heart filled with contentment as she gazed into Michael's love-filled eyes. "I guess that settles it, then," she whispered.

"I think so." His head descended, then he stopped and glanced at Lila. He grinned. "Just a quick kiss?"

Lila gave a curt nod.

Michael gave a contented sigh as his lips closed over Star's, and she knew the past was indeed gone. She looked forward to a glorious future.

A Letter To Our Readers

Dear Reader:

In order that we might better contribute to your reading enjoyment, we would appreciate your taking a few minutes to respond to the following questions. We welcome your comments and read each form and letter we receive. When completed, please return to the following:

Fiction Editor
Heartsong Presents
PO Box 719
Uhrichsville, Ohio 44683

1. Did you enjoy reading *But For Grace* by Tracey Victoria Bateman?
   ❑ Very much! I would like to see more books by this author!
   ❑ Moderately. I would have enjoyed it more if

   _____

   _____

   _____

2. Are you a member of **Heartsong Presents**? ❑ Yes ❑ No
   If no, where did you purchase this book? _____

   _____

3. How would you rate, on a scale from 1 (poor) to 5 (superior), the cover design? _____

4. On a scale from 1 (poor) to 10 (superior), please rate the following elements.

   ____ Heroine   ____ Plot
   ____ Hero   ____ Inspirational theme
   ____ Setting   ____ Secondary characters

5. These characters were special because?_____
_____
_____

6. How has this book inspired your life?_____
_____
_____

7. What settings would you like to see covered in future
   Heartsong Presents books? _____
_____
_____

8. What are some inspirational themes you would like to see
   treated in future books? _____
_____
_____

9. Would you be interested in reading other **Heartsong
   Presents** titles? ❏ Yes ❏ No

10. Please check your age range:
   ❏ Under 18   ❏ 18-24
   ❏ 25-34   ❏ 35-45
   ❏ 46-55   ❏ Over 55

Name_____
Occupation _____
Address _____
City_____ State_____ Zip_____

Gold Rush Christmas

*W*hen the "Gold Fever" epidemic sweeps the nation in 1849, people drop everything to chase the dream of striking it rich. Follow one family's itch for adventure from California to the Rockies to Alaska—and discover a Christmas gift more valuable than gold.

Four Christmases in gold country prove life's most priceless gifts come not in the form of polished gold—but from the vast riches of a loving heart.

Historical, paperback, 352 pages, 5 $\frac{3}{16}$"x 8"

❤ • ❤ • ❤ • ❤ • ❤ • ❤ ❤ ❤ • ❤ • ❤ • ❤ • ❤ • ❤

Please send me ____ copies of *Gold Rush Christmas* I am enclosing $6.99 for each. (Please add $2.00 to cover postage and handling per order. OH add 7% tax.)

Send check or money order, no cash or C.O.D.s please.

Name _____

Address_____

City, State, Zip _____

To place a credit card order, call 1-800-847-8270.
Send to: Heartsong Presents Reader Service, PO Box 721, Uhrichsville, OH 44683

❤ • ❤ • ❤ • ❤ • ❤ • ❤ ❤ ❤ • ❤ • ❤ • ❤ • ❤ • ❤

Presents

Great Inspirational Romance at a Great Price!

Heartsong Presents books are inspirational romances in contemporary and historical settings, designed to give you an enjoyable, spirit-lifting reading experience. You can choose wonderfully written titles from some of today's best authors like Peggy Darty, Sally Laity, Tracie Peterson, Colleen L. Reece, Debra White Smith, and many others.

When ordering quantities less than twelve, above titles are $3.25 each.
Not all titles may be available at time of order.